A House at Hill-Beauty

Dipak K Pal

First published in India 2010 by **Frog Books**
an imprint of **Leadstart Publishing Pvt Ltd**
1 Level, Trade Centre
Bandra Kurla Complex
Bandra (East) Mumbai 400 051 India
Telephone: +91-22-40700804
Fax: +91-22-40700800
Email: info@leadstartcorp.com
www.leadstartcorp.com / www.frogbooks.net

Marketing Office:
Unit: 122 / Building B/2
First Floor, Near Wadala RTO
Wadala (East) Mumbai 400 037 India
Phone: +91-22-24046887

US Office:
Axis Corp, 7845 E Oakbrook Circle
Madison, WI 53717 USA

ISBN No: 978-93-80154-38-1

Publisher and Managing Editor: Sunil K Poolani
Books Editors: Jake McPherson & Radhika Nair
Design Editor: Mishta Roy

Typeset in Book Antiqua
Printed at Manipal Technologies Limited, Manipal

Price — India: Rs 195; Elsewhere: US $12

in memory of my father

Paint the soul,
Never mind the legs and arms
– 'Fra Lippo Lippi', Robert Browning

About the Author

Dipak K Pal was born, in 1949, into a family which migrated from the erstwhile East Bengal. He worked as a college teacher in Orissa.

Dipak has published three novels, three collections of short stories, a collection of poems and literary essays in Oriya. His columns used to appear in *The Telegraph*, Calcutta, and recently Writers Workshop published his collection of poetry in English: *Remembrance of Rains Past*.

Now retired, Dipak presently lives in Bangalore with his wife and architect-son. He can be contacted at jgd_dkp1@rediffmail.com

Prologue

After my graduation, sitting quietly in my room, I used to scribble down leisurely anything that came to my mind. As a student, my literature teachers used to praise me for the creative flavour of my language. Some of them had even advised me to take up journalism as my career. One of them, who used to teach us vernacular literature, expressed his surprise that I never participated in any creative writing competition, nor would I contribute anything to the college magazine. He once asked me about it, and I also didn't know why it used to happen to me. I simply said that I didn't feel like it. The teacher then said that he wanted to know exactly that: why it was that I didn't feel like writing. I told him that it might be because I never liked fabrication. And, writing a story was nothing but fabrication. He said that fabrication was not the correct word. It would be rather a creative innovation. I told him that I was not interested in juggling words.

"Writing a story simply means that you are telling others about that which is not there in the world nor has it happened to you."

My teacher said, "Look, nothing exists in the world, unless you make it exist. Nothing happens to you, unless you make it happen to you. You see, just now a bus went by. You heard the sound, didn't you?" I nodded. My teacher then said, "Now go and ask that deaf boy if he heard the sound of the bus going by. He will ask you 'sound'? What is it? Won't he? So, you see, a thing exists, and at the same time it does not exist, too. Don't bother about it. You just make it happen, and that is creativity."

That was how he used to advise and encourage me to write. But, I never paid any heed to it. So, when after my graduation, I was passing my days idly, one day sitting in my lonely room, I felt very sad, and I didn't know why. It was then that the suggestion of my teacher flashed across my mind. I tried hard to understand what he had said. And, in the process of understanding, unconsciously I started scribbling on a piece of paper lying before me on the table. When I came to my awareness, I saw that I had written down something that could be called a story, and that it had in a vague way a representation of what could be described as the account of a refugee boy from East Bengal or something like that.

And, this is how The Story of My Birth came into being. It goes as follows:

The Story of My Birth

I feel overwhelmed when I look at this house. After all, everybody builds a house, invariably after his retirement. So did my father. He raised a house here at Hill-Beauty.

But, his raising of a house was different from the way others do it. Many years after, when I grew up, I realised that my father was not merely trying to build a house for shelter. It was much more than the usual construction of bricks and cement.

Over these years, I have seen it growing into a structure like a bud opening out into a full blossom. The house was a dream for my father. He wanted to bring this dream out of the vacuity of imagination and to plant it solidly on this earth.

I distinctly recall the day when I first set my foot here on this spot. It was cloudy. There was not much sunshine when I got off the bus with my father at a place marked for the weekly local market. It wasn't a market day, and that is perhaps why we were the two lone passengers to get down from the bus.

I felt thrilled, a little nervous, too, as though I were

just walking into a wonderland, Ahead, I could see only a vast stretch of an uneven barren land, dry and rocky, evoking the picture of a highwayman on a horse galloping across the rows of small hills at a distance.

The hills far away charmed me deeply, and I asked my father, "Is it the place where you are going to raise our house?"

My father gave a sigh and nodded. "Yes, my boy. This is the place for a fate-less man like me."

"Why do you say it like that, Baba, fate-less?" I protested. "It looks so lovely here! Those hills there! Oh, how I would like to climb them!"

"Yes, lovely. But, it's not hills I am used to, son. It's rivers I am used to. Only rivers. Rivers and rivers. You could see all around yourself it's only rivers and waters and sails and fish-nets and songs, the boatman's songs. You can't hear them anymore. They are gone."

I was going to ask about those songs when I saw my father fall silent.

A deep sigh again, and then my father held out his forefinger to me. "Let's walk down there. It seems you have come to like it so much!" he said.

That was how I first came over to this place where now stands this house, which my father dreamt and then started building; but it's strange that he could never take to this place - the hills around, the brown rocks, the patchy shrubs, and the vast stretch of the uneven barren land. But then, he decided in favour of it just because it was available at so cheap a price that he thought he could afford, and that day perhaps I came to know how my father had gone mad for getting settled. Settled in life: "You've got to get stuck to your earth. Only that is how you live," my father used to say.

On our way back home, we boarded an overcrowded bus, and there in the bus, it all took place. I saw my father jostling ahead to reach a seat just vacated by an elderly lanky man who rose to his feet perhaps to get down at the next stop. As he started moving toward the exit door I saw it happen. They – my father and the lanky man – were now standing face to face. Their eyes rolled over each other, and then I heard my father exclaim, "Sameer!" The bus came to a groaning halt, and the noisy bustle inside drowned the whole shower of exclamations coming from both of them. I was trying hard to recall the man when I felt my father reach for my hand and almost pulled me down onto the road along with that man whom he introduced to me minutes after as "Sameer *kaku* – do you recognise him?"

The name Sameer *kaku* instantly brought to my memory a pale picture of a man rushing for the train, the fringe of his white dhoti in one hand and a small black leather bag in the other.

The scene, I remember, used to make us laugh. I remember my younger sister also there by my side. We would exchange mischievous glances, feeling delighted at the scene. Once it so happened that I could not help myself and burst out laughing, which annoyed my father so much that he slapped my face hard. Overtaken by the whole situation, I could not cry nor could I grasp the sudden anger of my father.

Later in the night after we all had our meals, my mother came to set the mosquito net when she asked, sternly, "Why did you laugh at Sameer *kaku*? You're getting so unmannerly these days."

"But, Ma," I muttered to explain the whole comic air that Sameer *kaku* evoked when she rudely cut me short.

"Don't come up with excuses. You aren't a kid anymore like your sister."

I failed to get at my mother's rudeness, too. And, wondering what could be the whole mystery, I fell silent. My mother took my silence for sulkiness, and so she tried to make me understand.

"See, when you grow up you'll come to know how hard it is to live on this Earth. You don't know, too, it's all the more difficult when you're homeless, when you're uprooted from your land in the darkness of the night."

It was sometime later that day she started narrating the story of her frightful escape that also entailed the story of my birth on the rough wooden planks of a country boat. She was not able to recall the journey across the river so sharply, she would say, except the fact that it was precisely a salty smell that was irritating her nose throughout for the simple reason that the boat "we were sailing on was actually a fishing boat, and that was again because your Sameer *kaku* couldn't arrange anything else, and moreover was it possible to arrange anything in such a haste? In fact, instantly?"

"Why Ma? What was the hurry about?" I asked, to which my mother would keep her eyes shut. She would take a long pause. Perhaps she was trying to recollect the details, I used to think.

After a long silence she would say, "When your Sameer *kaku* came rushing in that evening, I was then wriggling in pain. You were in my womb. Your father felt so helpless that he was sitting there like a statue. Sameer *kaku* was in a fix. We have to move instantly, no other way, Sameer *kaku* said, they might set our house on fire any moment. Your father urged him to arrange anything possible for an immediate escape. And, that was how he managed to get one fishing boat, and we had to rush out immediately. I was struck with a strange sensation of terror and anxiety. We didn't even have time to take a last look at our house, and just as I got into the boat, my pain revived. I was lying on the wooden planks, unconscious."

"And then what happened, Ma?"

"And then? ... Then you were born."

And, so I was born in the story of my mother.

Sometimes, without any context, all of a sudden, my mother would say, "Know? I had a pair of geese in the pond in our backyard. I used to go to the pond to take a bath in the morning, to do my utensils, to wash clothes and all that, and then I would be talking to my geese. They were so fond of me! I don't know what they must be thinking of me?" My mother would go into silence.

After a while, she would say, "They must be still wondering what happened to me! No?"

***

It was this script that was lying there on my table for months, gathering dust. I had totally forgotten about it when one afternoon my friend, my intimate friend, had come to the room, and as I was not home, my friend started browsing through my scribbling casually, just to pass the time, and in the process read it over and over again.

When I returned home, it was almost evening. My friend said, "Congratulations!"

I was at a loss to understand what it was for. So I asked, surprised, "What for?"

"For the wonderful beginning."

"Of what?"

"Of your story."

"Oh! That one! But, I was not writing any story?"

"I know. It was not a story. What is it then?"

I didn't know either what it was. So, I kept mum.

My friend asked, "Was it life, if not story?"

That, I also had no idea about. So again, I kept mum.

My friend then said, "You know I am doing my postgraduate in literature? So, I can tell you what it is. It is a fiction. Okay?"

I looked at my friend, failing to understand the import of such a long prelude.

My friend continued, "I liked it, the beginning of it, I mean. I liked it very much. I appreciate your style also. Fantastic. And, there lies the point. You know I am doing my postgraduate in literature, and as a student of literature, I would like to make some critical comments on it. Would you like me to?"

I said, "Okay, carry on."

My friend said, "Fine. That's like a good boy. And even if you won't like, I don't mind. You know, I am doing literature?"

We smiled at each other, and then my friend resumed, "Yes, I was talking about your style. Fantastic. It's really fantastic. But, don't think that I am praising you. I mean the style of your writing. I am just making a critical observation, you see, quite objectively, that what you have written reads like a fantasy."

I interrupted, "What is that?"

"What that?"

"That. You're Fantasy?"

My friend gave a mischievous smile and said, "Oh yes, fantasy. You don't know what it is. Well then, let me explain it. First, a Fantasy is, you know, a fantasy, I mean not real, I mean something not happening actually."

I again interrupted, "Bogus. How can things actually happen when what you are writing is a fiction?"

My friend, sitting in a thoughtful pose with the cheek resting on his forefinger and his head tilting slightly towards the left, said, "The point you raised is a relevant one. There is logic in it. But, well-well, I remember now, and you know I have the habit of forgetting what I read. Well, I remember, it is written in the book that a fantasy is that which is not located in historical time and place, and the moment you locate your story in a historical time and place it becomes realism. The way you have written your story it doesn't appear to be realistic. It smacks of fantasy."

I listened intently to what my friend was saying and then I started laughing loudly, saying, "You are really fantastic. You are calling history as fantasy! Ha! Ha! Ha! It's history man, History! History! History of our partition." As I was laughing, my friend's face got wrinkled. My friend sulked, and my most intimate friend then silently slipped away from the room, ignoring my requests to stay.

Weeks later, coming back home one evening, I saw my friend seriously going through the manuscript of The Story of my Birth, undisturbed, even at my footsteps. As I sat on my cot, I could hear his voice, "What is that history you were talking about?"

"Oh! History?" I said, "History of partition."

"Which partition?" My friend asked innocently.

I said, "Stupid, you don't know the partition? Partition of India? India and Pakistan?"

My friend turned round and looking straight at me said, "Ha! Read about it somewhere. I haven't much idea about it. It's just that as I remember I have read that on the eve of our independence India was divided into two countries on the basis of religion and that it resulted in violent riots and massive bloodshed and all that. Okay, it is there in the history books. But what has it got to do with your story? I just don't understand."

I said, "You can't. You are just a bookworm. For you, life means books."

My friend got annoyed and said, "Hey! Don't say it like that. It's you who started with history and all that nonsense."

I too felt peeved and answered, "Look, you simply can't dismiss history as nonsense. It is because of the history that the characters in my story were uprooted from their native lands, and that is the beginning of their tragedy. I was writing a story of an uprooted family, the tragedy part of it, I mean."

"All bogus!" My friend said, "As if tragedy doesn't happen otherwise."

I said, "Yes, it might be happening. But, that is not my concern. I am concerned with how it is a particular piece of history..."

Before I could complete my sentence, my friend shouted me stop, "Fuck your history! History! History! History! As if there is no tragedy without history?"

Then there was absolute silence. In the silence, my friend slipped away from the room.

After that unfortunate incident, we didn't meet for a long time. The next time we met, strangely, we both were in a jolly mood. My friend asked, "What happened to your story? You haven't progressed any more?"

I said, "No."

"Why?"

"Don't know," I replied.

My friend got close to me and in a soft, cajoling tone said, "I would like you to carry on with it. The only thing is that it should be credible. I mean, forget about that bogus stuff of realism, fantasy, history and all that nonsense. What I mean is that when you read you must feel as if it is happening to you. You see, as a person I am not interested in what happened in history or what happens to anybody else. I am interested in only what happens to me, and" after a pause, he said, "To you."

I felt confused at this. How can one write only about

himself? And moreover why should one be interested in one's personal matter? And, how could it at all be called literature?

My friend smiled and said, "Don't stuff your mind with any humbug theories. What I mean is tell the story as if it is your own."

"But how?" I asked my friend.

He said, "Why, just make it appear like your autobiography? You are to tell your own life history, not anybody else's history. That will impress."

I explained, "I think perhaps that is what I have done. It was in the first person."

My friend said, "No, a mere first person won't do. And moreover, it read like a fairy tale, or something like what happens in a dream, something like ...like...well, I don't know what it was like. The fact is you are to make it happen to your own life, something like that."

"But how?"

My friend pondered a bit and then said, "Well, I have an idea...Give it the title 'My Autobiography.' It will solve the problem."

I gave it a thought, and then it struck me that I had already given it a title "The House at Hill-Beauty." I told my friend so.

"Doesn't matter. Now you start 'My Autobiography.'

I asked how that could be. A novel must have one title, not two at a time.

My friend argued, "Why do you think that you are writing a novel?"

"Then what?" I asked.

My friend said, "Nothing, just a book."

And this was the genesis of my Book.

One

My father died in heavy rains.

I was then two hundred miles away. One day a telegram came that said "father's condition critical." With the red-coloured telegram paper in my hand, I looked up at the sky. An overcast sky. Overcast with thick, black clouds.

It was the blackness of the clouds that struck me. There were silver lines though, cutting across the black clouds, emitting a bit of dim sunshine. It was already past noon, but the atmosphere wore an unusually sad look. Might be because there was no bright sunshine. Might be because the telegram all of a sudden made me sad.

Not that the telegram shocked me. Since the day my father was admitted to the medical college hospital, I was certain someday news of this sort would reach me two hundred miles away, where I was staying then. It was months back, perhaps six or so, when he took to bed, ill. The day he fell ill, incidentally, I was at home. First, it was a low fever, somewhere between 99 or 100 degrees. I took it as a mild illness, but strangely, a kind of unease seized me. Towards the evening the temperature was on the rise. I immediately rushed for a doctor. Strangely again, the doctor, a close acquaintance of my father, ignored my anxiety. In fact, he laughed away my uneasiness about the whole situation and, with laughter loud enough to fill the room, diagnosed it as a symptom of a seasonal flu, which, as he explained me, had recently tended to manifest unusually and inexplicably with a high temperature. When I came back with the medicine, I saw my father lying still on the bed, and my mother was in the kitchen like she would be seen at this time any other day.

She simply asked: "What did the doctor say?"

"Nothing, simple flu."

Mother said, "I also thought so." I did not say anything. It was just that I was wondering why I wasn't able to see the things as everybody else was.

In the middle of the night, I found the temperature was alarmingly high. It unnerved me terribly. I couldn't remember a day I had seen my father ill. Even a day of mild cough or cold was difficult to remember. The whole night I stayed awake gripped by an unknown fear. The kind of fear my mother used to talk about in her story of my birth.

The next morning, my father went into a state of coma. And then, I felt normal. Everybody in and around my house looked at me with utter surprise. They all appeared disturbed, worried, anxious, sad, helpless, and visibly perturbed. I was the only one among them who looked composed. My mother, when she knew about Father's coma, stayed at the edge of his bed like she was stuck. The world around her was lost, she felt. She didn't respond to anybody, anything. She fell silent. Coolly, I went to the nearby hospital. On the way, I came across the same doctor. I told him what had happened. He nonchalantly advised me to arrange an ambulance for my father to get him admitted in the hospital. It was when I told him that I was going exactly for that he gave me an intent look. The cool on my face perhaps disturbed him deeply.

He said, "You better come with me. I will see to it. They'd harass you."

For two months or so, my father was there in that hospital with pipes in his nose, mouth, and the genitals. Occasionally, when someone whispered into his ear, he would seem to nod. Those were the moments of immense joy for everybody. For the days following or even sometimes for weeks together, all would be talking about those moments with a clear sign of happiness on their faces. Even the doctors too. They'd rather explain it as the clear indication of improvement. And, that kept us hoping for a miracle. Day after day, week after week, month after month.

It was one morning I casually asked the doctor, "Father is alive. No?"

The reply came pat, "Why don't you shift him to the medical college hospital?"

The next day he was moved to the medical college hospital. He lay there on his bed with acute bedsores on his back for, I imagine, not less than four months. Four months he lived on his sore back with no complaint or expression of pain. He was not in his right senses. And that was how we all had forgotten about his death. The very idea of his death seemed to be ridiculous. On one such day, I do not know why, I whispered into his ear, "Baba, don't worry. I will complete your half-raised house." And, that was it! Amazing! I saw a pale smile spreading over his chin. I even thought his eyes shone. That night, when I was coming back to my place leaving him in the care of my younger sister's husband, suddenly a fear seized me. He was going to die, anytime now.

So, when the telegram ultimately came just after a couple of days, I was not surprised. Even though the death was not explicit in the telegram, I knew it was. And that, in fact, surprised me. What does death mean for my father now after lying on a bed-sore back for four months? Without hearing, without seeing, without feeling, without talking, without listening...and it struck me that perhaps it was so. He couldn't die because his mind was still hooked to his dream, his house, and the half-raised structure of his house. The moment I told him that I would complete it, his mind got off its hook.

And he died.

The thought filled me with guilt. I could have told him so much earlier! I could imagine the pain he must be undergoing inside without its expression on his face. I could have saved him from this pain, I thought.

The guilt hung heavily on me all the way from my place to the railway station. It was even in the clouds above. I stood on queue, a long one, for the ticket without realising that almost an hour had passed in the meantime. When I entered the platform, the torrential rain came. Rains started pouring down. And, that heavy shower melted the guilt in me, the news of my father's death. I boarded the train and luckily got a seat by the window. It was still raining. The rain-washed earth outside looked so hazy through the glass. The world looked like a mass of clouds. Even the rains were not visible. Looking outside, it was difficult to know if the train was moving at all. All the while, I was only looking outside. Blankly.

I came to my senses only when the train had halted at a junction for a long time, and it was not known whether the train would move from this station at all. I asked the man sitting next to me why. He said that it was because of the rain. For the last two days, the track ahead was completely under water. The two major rivers, the Mahanadi and the Kathjodi, had already started overflowing. The man sitting in front of me added that the next small station had been washed away.

So, it came to this: there was no possibility of the train moving further.

But, it suddenly started moving. Everybody around me looked surprised.

And more surprises were in store. In the middle of the sky, the clouds too started clearing. The fields, the trees, and the small hills at a distance submerged in sprawling water gradually appeared, glistening with bright sunshine. As I was looking intently at the shining sunshine reflecting on the floodwaters, the man sitting in front of me muttered something. I thought he asked me something, and so when withdrawing my eyes from the sparkling open scene outside, I straightaway threw a look at him.

He said, "No, I was just wondering if the train would be moving ahead smoothly."

"Why?"

The man said, "They say tracks have been washed away."

I asked, "Where?"

He replied. "That I don't know." And then, perhaps because my tone had betrayed an unusual anxiety, the man followed up with the question, "Where are you supposed to go? Is it so urgent?"

It was then only that the thought of the death of my father came back again. But, this time it was not so much the death of my father as rather the very state of his being alive, alive (if one could express it so) on his back with the unbearable pain of the bed-sores, not some days or weeks but for as long as four months, solely and passionately, only to hear what I had ultimately said..."Baba, don't worry. I will complete your half-raised house." I also remembered the day when he had taken me first to show me the place he was dreaming to raise his house. He told me that day, "One has got to belong to somewhere." And, I know somewhere for him was essentially somewhere on this Earth. "One has got to get stuck to this earth." That was how he used to put his dream across. A sense of belonging.

A house for my father was an expression for this sense of belonging. Unless one belongs to, he cannot go away also. My father was not able to leave this Earth, because he wanted to be sure that he belonged to it. And, I regret that I delayed in feeding him with that sense. The sense of belonging.

Suddenly with an alarming jerk the train again came to a halt. It was not even a station, nor was one within the visible distance. The passengers inside first started craning their heads out through the windows and doors, trying to see what had happened. Nothing could be seen clearly. Failing to ascertain the reason, everybody then started talking about the washed away tracks that they had heard others talking about. After half an hour or so, the passengers saw the driver and the guards of the train loitering on the track. The railway track was on raised ground, and that is perhaps why it was saved from the floodwater here. Down the grade, wherever you looked it was only water and water.

There was no sign of the train moving soon. It was even doubtful whether it would move at all. I saw that my compartment had almost become empty. Along with others, I too got down from the train, and it was then that the scene struck me. Most of the passengers were looking at a crowd down below, a curious crowd, some sitting, some standing with gaping mouths, some talking with each other in undertones, some looking blankly at God knew where. What was most surprising about the whole scene was the silence. A hushed atmosphere.

Some of the enthusiastic passengers of our train in the meantime had walked down to the spot, and as they climbed back to the track, they delivered very interesting news that it was a case of suicide.

"Suicide?" Someone asked. "Who? Why?"

The questions were so stupid that it evoked boisterous laughter, and the man coming straight from the spot also joined the laughter and said, "How can I know who it was?"

The man asking the stupid question murmured, "No, I just wanted to know if he was an old man or a woman or a young man or a girl or a bride."

The man coming from the spot this time put up a rather sober look and said, "Yes, it was an old man. He hanged himself from a tree."

Someone else asked, "Know why?"

By this time, there had been another gathering here on the railway track. The man from the spot threw a smiling glance at the small crowd around him and clearing his throat said, "Yes, as I gathered from the villagers, it is very interesting. The old man has an unemployed son who wanted to go in for business, and he had arranged a handsome loan from a bank, for which he egged on his father to put their homestead land on the mortgage. The father was resisting strongly but ultimately gave in when the son threatened that otherwise he was going to commit suicide."

"So finally, it was the old father who committed suicide!" Someone commented in a mocking tone.

The man from the spot said, "Yes, it was just a day before yesterday that, as they said, the father went along with his son to the bank with the land deed wrapped in a polythin paper lest it be spoiled in the rain, and this morning he was seen hanging from the tree."

There followed a moment of silence. All stood speechless. Perhaps nobody could decide how to react to such a situation. True, the man committing suicide was a stranger to all of us. But then, it was after all a death, and that too not a normal or natural death. Moreover, the crowd smelt something like a dramatic conflict in the whole story of it: the conflict of a familiar nature between father and son, the clash of attitudes between two generations, old and the new. In fact, it was this dramatic element that finally redeemed the crowd from the bizarre silence. Most strangely, it was not any young man, rather a quite old man among us who broke the silence with a terse muttering: "Idiot." He uttered the word as if he was trying to crush a betel nut in between his teeth. All eyes now fell on that old man.

Someone asked, "What do you mean? Who was the idiot? The son?"

The old man strongly nodded his head, "No. The old father."

There ensued an exchange of dialogue then.

"Father? How come!"

"Why? Who else could it be?"

"The son."

"Son? How?"

"Because, the son was a rogue, trying to exploit the sentiment of a father."

"Yes, a rogue the son might be. But, the idiot is his old father."

"That is what I am asking. Why?"

"Because, for that bloody old man, a piece of land was more valuable than his own son, the future of his son!"

The drama was ongoing. I tried to evade the whole scene there on the track. It was simply because, I don't know why, it pained me a lot to hear people accusing the old father of inordinate importance he had given to his homestead rather than to his unemployed son, of behaving like an idiot. I started withdrawing from that crowded scene on the track, and my eyes fell on the sight at a distance below.

The sun in the meantime had gone behind the gathering clouds. The glittering sunshine on floodwaters around was steadily getting dim. The weather was again getting heavier. In the fading sunshine, I could faintly see a figure hanging from the tree. And by the time I came to my senses, I found myself standing in front of that hanging figure, in the midst of a strange crowd staring at me. I wanted to take a look at the face of the dead father, but it was covered with a white piece of cloth, perhaps to hide the grimace from other's view, especially children or women. A feeling then ran through me: Is it possible to see if the eyes of the dead father are focused on the earth? The land? So dear to him, even dearer than his offspring?

And, driven by that feeling, I stupidly moved closer to the hanging figure when someone pointed at me and asked the man standing by his side, "Is this fellow that bastard son?" The man asked so loudly and with so much loathing in his raucous voice that it made me halt instantly, and my whole body even started trembling terribly. It struck me that I would certainly get beaten up, if they mistook me to be the son responsible for the suicide. And then, God saved me when I saw that the passengers of our train were scurrying towards their compartment, and I saw that one of them, perhaps the man sitting in front of me in the compartment, was waving has hands at me. As I waved back, he shouted at me to hurry up. The train was about to move. With the slushy mud splashed up to my knee when I reached there gasping, the train had already begun to move. I somehow caught hold of the outstretched hand of the man and found myself safe in the compartment, and as it happens to me always, I felt so choked with gratitude that I could not even say thank you. I just smiled and gave him a deep look. He also smiled back.

The train by then had regained its usual speed. The man in front asked, "You saw the old man hanging?" I nodded. "You seemed to be very curious," he said.

I said, "No, it is just that suddenly I remembered my father."

The man got inquisitive and hesitantly asked, "Your father? Why? I mean your father is alive, no?"

I said, "No, he is dead."

The man was apologetic and took pity on me and said, "I am sorry." I fell silent, the man, too.

Moments after, he broke the silence, "If you don't mind, did your father commit suicide…I mean if…"

I calmly said, "No, he didn't."

The man said, "I am sorry. How did he die?"

I couldn't immediately decide what to say. In fact, I had no precise idea about his illness. I knew only that he was in a state of coma for a long time. But then, coma cannot be the cause of the illness.

It was when I was trying to make out the cause of my father's death the man asked another question, "How long is he dead?" This time I was really at a loss. When did he die exactly? Yesterday? Today morning? And, moreover, is he really dead?

In my puzzlement I said, "The fact is…I mean…I am not sure, but I am certain he is dead."

The man looked at me sharply, intently, and with a sheer sense of disbelief in his eyes, was almost trying to scan my whole being. I could understand his situation and said, coolly, "The fact is, only this morning I got the telegram that his condition is critical." I paused, not knowing what more to say.

"And later, you got the information?" the man asked.

"About what?" I asked.

"About your father's death?" the man said.

I said, "No, I haven't yet."

This time also I replied coolly, and that was what surprised the man. Perhaps he felt utterly stupefied and so didn't like to carry on the conversation. He just stayed gazing at me.

I said, " In fact, a couple of days back when I returned from the medical college hospital, I could sense that he was sure to be relieved, either of his death or of his life." I didn't know why instead of stating the fact straight, I was using language that was helping more to camouflage rather than disclose the fact and that perhaps led the man to doubt my sanity. I rightly guessed it and thought that I must speak out as plainly as possible. So, I added, "Before

I left the medical hospital, I had whispered into my father's ears that I would complete the house he had started building, and when I told him that, I saw his face light up."

I stopped and looked at the man. He fixed his eyes on me and perhaps was trying to make sense out of what I was saying. This time however he said, "I see! He fell ill before he could finish the construction of his house and was obsessed with it. Is it so?"

I said, "Yes, obsessed he was, certainly. But then, it was more than an obsession, something like, you can say, passion. A passion that a man lives for, that makes one feel the relevance of living, the meaning of life, the significance of being born, born on this earth, on this planet...." I held my breath for a while. Suddenly, I could feel that I was getting philosophical and must be looking like a sentimental idiot. I blushed and turned my eyes away.

The man put it precisely. "It seems the house meant everything to your father. No?" I gave a passive nod. He asked, "But why?"

I said, "Because, we don't have a house."

"How come you don't have a house? Strange!"

I simply repeated, "Yes, we don't have a house."

My talk this time was so plain and simple and so true to the heart that it made no sense to the man. I thought perhaps such facts are not to be transmitted so nakedly. To make it comprehensible, it needs to be packaged in philosophy. We understand philosophy better than the bare facts of life.

After a long pause the man asked, "Where did your father belong to?"

I said, "Nowhere."

The man looked at me sharply and asked, "No, what I mean is where is your native place?"

I said, "Nowhere." The answer came pat, involuntarily. Perhaps because, anything else than that would have involved a lot of explanations such as how is it that one doesn't have an ancestral house, and how it is that we don't belong to it, and how can one's separation from his ancestral place be irreversible, and so many other queries, too. In order to just avoid such embarrassing situations, I thought of an evasive answer and so said, "Nowhere."

We both, then, fell silent. The man was not able to understand me. I, too, could not explain the facts properly. I tried hard to put everything clearly and simply but failed. So, both of us slowed down our talk to an intermittent exchange of funny gestures and ultimately went into silence.

Silence has its own impact. Somehow or other, the man took me to be an eccentric fellow, and as we normally tend to behave with such a person by trying to avoid or ignore, the man slowly withdrew his attention from me. First, he unfolded the newspaper in his hands and hid his face behind it and never looked back at me.

I welcomed the scene and the silence. The train was running at its usual speed now, and a liquid darkness had started shadowing the atmosphere over the watery land. The silence was deepening by the rhythmic rumble of the running train. At a far distance, I could see a pale, hazy moon trying to wriggle out of the rain-washed sky casting a misty charm over the shadowy land. I felt nostalgic and a lumpy sadness in my throat.

The silence took me back to my father again. It was about the day he returned from Calcutta. He had been back there after many years, and it was then that my mother reminded him of Sameer *kaku*. "If at all you're going to Calcutta, please, try to find out the whereabouts of our *thakur-po*. What has happened to him? No news! No appearance! Nothing! He didn't seem to be a person who would stay silent for years together!" In fact, over those years, we had neither heard of nor seen Sameer *kaku*, and it was very strange. At my mother's pushiness, father made inquiries at the place of *kaku*'s fish-business and was greatly disheartened to learn that *kaku* had still been in that business and had been coming to the place as usual. My father kept the news secret from my mother and instead lied to her that *kaku* had already packed up his business and had left no address.

Perhaps, I knew why it had happened so. I remember,

one day, in my presence, how my father sighed over his fate that he could not give education to his children in their own language, since, during the partition, my father had migrated to this state where people speak in a different language, and he regretted Sameer *kaku*'s news that he had already bought a piece of land in Calcutta and was about to start the construction of his house. Perhaps Sameer *kaku* feared that father would send us to his house for our education at Calcutta and that fear might have prompted him to distance himself from us and stay silent.

Sometimes, I also used to wonder at the behaviour of Sameer *kaku*. What was it that made him so unkind to us! To my mother! As I remember from the tale of my mother's story of my birth, Sameer *kaku* was certainly not a person like that. He had saved my father. He had saved my mother. He had saved us. Our whole family. But now, he was trying to severe all contacts with us.

In those days, because of my tender age or maybe because I was too inexperienced to grasp the ways of the world, I felt terribly annoyed when my father, on his return from Calcutta, told my mother, "Yes, I met Sameer. But, he is no more that Sameer. He has changed. He has changed completely, completely, completely changed!" As he was saying, he broke down in tears and my mother was literally taken aback.

She could only say, "No. No. How could it be?" I had noticed how her eyes were getting bigger and bigger in utter disbelief.

For the days that followed, a whole week or so, mother kept herself totally withdrawn, silent, sometimes looking blankly at the trees in our courtyard or at the pot on the cooking fire with rice boiling in it.

One could feel a crematory silence in our home all those days. No one, neither my father nor my mother, had ever imagined that Sameer *kaku* could behave with us in such a way, to speak the truth, so selfishly, and so cruelly, too, in order that his own interest of taking care of his own family would not be affected.

But now, I understand why Sameer *kaku* behaved like

that. Now, I can understand the intricate relationship between social life and the economics of our day-to-day living. Uprooted from one's own land, of a secure and leisurely life, it was naturally the instinct of survival that counted more than the social relationship.

Not that my father, with his experience and age, was unaware of such a practical knowledge, but even then, he felt so upset that he also stayed withdrawn for days together. And, it was in those days of his great disappointment that he decided to possess a piece of land and a house of his own. Perhaps he felt that the relationship with a man was subject to change but not with the land or the house. A desire for sticking to. Attaching oneself to something durable and rendering thereby the meaning of life. Yes, I am living for this. This is the purpose of my life. That this is how I belong to this earth. This is why I was born. I am not nobody. I am somebody. It was that passion which still made my father breathe, lying on the hospital bed, even though he was not aware of what was happening around him or even the fact that he was still alive.

Now, with the rumble of the train, it dawned on me that I should have put out that passion in him and could have saved him from the unbearable pain of lying there with bed-sores on his back for months and months. I should have whispered into his ears, "Baba, I will complete your half-raised house."

I could have. I could have. I should have told him so much, much earlier!

With tears of remorse in my eyes, I tried to look out into a hazy moonlit land that was constantly slipping away from the view. I came to consciousness at the voice of the man in front.

"If I am not wrong, you are going for the last rites of your father?" I looked at the man and nodded my head. This time, he took pity on me and asked, "Do you know anybody there in the hospital? Anybody known to you intimately?" I shook my head in the negative. "Then you would be in difficulty," he said. I simply gave a resigned look. The man said: "If you don't mind, I will give you an address of someone who stays close by. You take my name, and he will help you."

He took out a pen from his pocket and asked for a piece of paper. I didn't have anything in my pocket except the ticket and a few currency notes of small denomination. It was then that a strange fear gripped me: How was I going to get the dead body discharged from the hospital and arrange the necessary rites for cremation with this meager amount in my pocket? Under the mid-day cloudy sky when I came out for the railway station to day, with the red-colored telegram crumpled in my palm, I had thought little of the need for money in such a situation. My mind itself was so clouded then. I looked at the man in front with an utter blankness. For a moment, the idea of asking for some money from him flashed across my mind. In the meantime, he had torn off a piece from the newspaper and was trying hard against the swaying motion of the train to write down the name and address of his friend. He did it finally and, raising his head, handed over the piece of paper to me. I took it from his outstretched hand gratefully. As I was shoving the slip into my pocket, a strange thought again struck me: If need be, I would rather borrow from his friend there. The next moment, I felt ashamed of my thought and to hide the feeling I turned my face away from the man in front, instead of expressing my gratitude more vocally and with gestures. Perhaps he felt piqued at my strange behaviour. It was very much visible on his face. I noticed it at a glance.

The man got down at a place previous to my stop. With the luggage in his hand, he raised himself from the seat and started making for the door. I could sense that he was to get down. So, I also got up, spontaneously, and, I don't know why, I bade him good-bye in a very traditional way with hands folded against my chest and saying "*Namaskar*." It surprised him. He was struck by the sudden change in my manner, and he also seemed to have been impressed by my politeness and the regard I showed. Patting me on the shoulder, he said some formal, consolatory words, genuinely.

I got down at the next station. The clock on the

platform told me it was already mid-night. I came out and stood in the open. It was drizzling, negligibly though. But, what was alarming for me was the darkness. Because of the unusual showers, the electrical supply had been disturbed, and the whole town was draped in utter darkness. Off the platform, it was almost lonely. I could hardly locate one or two passengers, at a distance, under the shade of an abandoned tea-stall, also looking for a rickshaw or even a human companion. They could see me by the flash of a passing car, as I did them. The car sped off, and there was darkness again. For a moment, when I was thinking of staying back at the station till dawn, a flash from a flashlight fell on me, and looking back, I saw a man coming out from the platform. As he came near, I asked him if he was to go towards the hospital.

The man said, "Yes, you can come along with me." He came nearer, and I saw a pockmarked, bearded, ebony-black rough face. I felt frightened for a moment, but there was no time to decide. The man asked me but didn't wait for my reply. He kept on walking. I started running behind him helplessly so that I could keep pace with him.

He asked, "Where are you supposed to go towards the hospital?"

I said, "The hospital itself."

Then, he wanted to know if any of my relations had been admitted there.

I said, "Yes, my father," and I fumbled. "But, he is dead". It was then only that the man looked at me. I said, "He was admitted months back, and it was only today that I got the telegram about his death." The man slowed down his pace.

It was still drizzling. We were almost soaked. The darkness had deepened the silence. We both were walking silently. After a long time, the man started talking, "Young man, you do not know that you are in the midst of a terrible night. For a long time in your life, I think, you will not be able to wipe this night from your memory." He paused, and I started trembling in fear. I was going to be robbed! I didn't mind being robbed, but if murdered! And strangely, it was not my imminent death that terrified me, but what struck me was the dead body of my father. It would rot and putrefy there at the hospital. If I were murdered, what would happen to my father? I didn't know whether I uttered those words or simply thought them, but first, I started sobbing and then started crying. The man walking with me stopped, surprised at my sudden outburst.

With the flashlight in his right hand, he put his left hand on my shoulder, patted it, and said softly, "Have patience." He repeated it again and again, "Have patience. Have Patience." He was perhaps under the impression that the thought of my father's death made me cry and so was trying to console me. The tenderness in his voice, contrary to his rough face, touched me. My fear was gone. He started walking again, and I tried to keep pace with him.

Occasionally, a stray dog would bark at our footsteps, breaking the silence. Sometimes one or two rickshaws would pass by us tinkling in the darkness. Otherwise, there was absolute silence.

The man then broke the silence and resumed his talk. "As I was saying, it is a terrible night. Perhaps you do not know why." He didn't wait for my reply. "Do you have any idea about the situation of this place now? Of this town at the moment?" He still didn't expect me to say anything. "You landed up here just now. How could you then know what the situation is? The situation is very grim. The whole town is in danger, the danger of being washed away." I stopped. He stopped, too, and said, "Do you want to see what you are walking on?" Saying this, he bent down and lifted his slippers in his hand and asked me also to take off my sandals and to walk barefoot. By that time, I was certain that I had run across a completely eccentric person, tending to insanity. But then, I had to go to the hospital to do the last rites for my father. At the moment, I was thinking of my father lying alone, though dead. I was coming under the grip of an unknown feeling, a feeling bundled in guilt, sadness, compassion, fear, and a vague sense of blankness. So, I had no other way but to oblige the eccentric man. Taking off my sandals, I held them in my hand and started walking bare feet.

After covering a considerable distance, the man asked, "Don't you feel anything under your feet? Do you ever feel that you are walking on a pukka road of a town?" I couldn't follow the import of his question and so kept mum. He then stood still, focused the light on the ground and asked me to press my feet down on the earth. I did so, not out of any curiosity, but out of a sheer fear and prayed for the scene to be over as soon as possible so that I could get to the hospital. I again felt worried for my father.

The man was excited and asked, "Do you see? See, how it is seeping! You just press hard and see how the water is oozing out!" He himself then started pressing his feet hard on the earth, and yes, I could see what he had been talking about. The ground was seeping. But then, I couldn't understand what was alarming about it. The man perhaps could read my mind. He put on his slippers and asked me to do so also. And then, as he started walking, he resumed his talk, "This morning, the river had already started overflowing its banks at many spots. It had crossed the danger level last midnight. And by this time, can you imagine, the entire town would have been washed away! Its tall buildings would have been submerged under the river Mahanadi." He then paused to take a deep breath. A cold shiver ran through my whole body. My God! What would have happened to my father! He would have also been washed away in the overflowing water! My God! I just couldn't think further. Now I realise how all the while I was thinking of my father as if he was still living and I was going to meet him.

The man looked at me with a mysterious smile and asked, "You didn't want to know why I then said it is a terrible night?"

Strangely, the instant reply came from me, "No, I was simply thinking of my father."

This time, the man didn't look at me but smiled in the same way and said, "Look at the houses on the road side or at a distance, everywhere. All closed, lights off, silent. Nobody seen outside, no anxiety, no fear, everybody in deep sleep. All is quiet." A pause, and then, "But, the scene was completely different just this evening. All were under the grip of a terrible fear. The way the water level of the river was rising was more than alarming. It was a scene of fear and panic. People were frantic about making a space for them and their luggage on the rooftops of high-rise buildings. From the panic of the evening to the peace of the night! How? I know you are going to ask. But, listen to what I say as the answer." He stopped and looked at me, and by that time, I had also raised my head to look at him and so our eyes met. This time I had really developed an interest in what he was saying. And, I noticed something in those sharp eyes. What it was exactly, I do not know, but it impressed me very much.

I listened to him intently: "Panic is still there, but the scene has merely shifted from this town to the low lying villages on the outskirts. By now, fifteen to twenty villages must have been overtaken by the sudden deluge. The authorities decided in the evening to dig open the embankment at those places so that you now see a silent peaceful night around you." He stopped, surveyed all around, and then started smiling, muttering on his own, "Strange is the way of the world!"

The man then suddenly went into a mysterious silence. As we walked on, I could hear only the sound of our own footsteps in the deadly silence of the dark night. When we were coming close to the hospital, it was still drizzling a little. The man again broke the silence and asked, "Here, we are. What do you plan to do?" I couldn't understand the import of his question and so looked at him foolishly. In the darkness, it might not have been possible for him to read the expression on my face, but my silence was perhaps more eloquent for he said, "What I mean is do you have anybody else here to help you? You alone can't do everything, particularly in this dark night. Either you'll have to wait till daybreak, or..." he paused and then lowering his tone asked, "In fact, when exactly did your father die? At what time? Do you have any knowledge of it?"

It was then for the first time since I got the telegram, suddenly, strangely, I started crying loudly like a child, and taking pity on me, the man tried to console me by patting me on my shoulder. I wailed louder, as if the whole of my pent up emotions broke open the riverbanks of my heart violently and started overflowing. The cry was so grotesquely loud that the watchman of the hospital rushed to us, and both of them had a tough time to console me.

They led me to the medicine ward and asked me to sit on a rickety wooden bench lying in the deserted corridor, and the watchman was kind enough to offer his help. He took the man along with him to the attendant on duty to enquire about my father.

I was sitting there alone in the eerie silence of the deserted corridor of the hospital, lit dimly by a candle in the corner. With the flame of the candle flickering in the occasional breeze, the shadowy light swayed on the dirty walls. The atmosphere looked so bizarre and ghostly that I felt frightened, and I sprang up. The rickety wooden bench creaked so weirdly that my feet got stuck there in fear. I failed to stir even an inch. And then, suddenly, my eyes fell on an abandoned table to my left in the dark of the lonely corridor on which, in between the flickers of the candle, I glimpsed something lying covered by a white cloth. It struck me that it could be a dead body, and my whole body started shaking.

I was saved from the situation when I saw them coming back towards me. The man who accompanied me so long reached me first and pointing at that table said, "Listen, you won't have to face much difficulty. Here is your father already released from the morgue."

"No!" I didn't scream at the top of my lungs but my voice appeared so strange that all of them were taken aback. Immediately, I said in a normal voice, "How could it be my father? It's a dead body!" They stood dumbstruck, sensing that I was deeply overtaken by grief.

The attendant exchanged a look with the man accompanying me, and the man, nodding his head, held my hand and led me to that table, saying softly, "Look, you are simply to identify the dead body and put some signatures on the papers so that he would release the dead body. We will do the rest. You needn't worry." I was still mute and stood at the table motionless, like a stone. The man laid his hand on my shoulder and said, "I understand the state of mind you are in. I realise your situation, but, you see, certain formalities are to be got over with." He then carefully held the fringe of the white cloth covering the dead body and slowly started uncovering the face.

The face was uncovered. And, yes, I saw that it was the face of my father. He was dead.

By the time we reached the cremation ground, it was past midnight, almost approaching dawn. The man accompanying me advised that the dead body had to be cremated before daybreak. "Otherwise, it is said that it would turn stale and the funeral rites then become meaningless since the soul could not be released from the body in due time, and in that case, the soul of the deceased suffers from pain, and because of the unbearable pain, it might turn wicked."

So, he took upon himself the responsibility of arranging everything in the midst of the darkness of that horrible night. First, he got a taxi with an unwilling, drowsy driver who was rude enough to say that he was not going to touch the dead body anyhow. In the meantime, my brother-in-law had arrived, and so, the man shoved some currency into the clammy palms of the attendant and the watchman and took their help along with my brother-in-law in carrying the dead body down to the taxi. I was asked to open the other door of the taxi and to get into it. As I did so, the man accompanying me held the head and the neck of my father and tried to push it into the taxi and asked me to hold the shoulder and pull the whole dead body onto the seat. I tried hard but could drag down only a part of it. It was so inconvenient there to keep one's feet steady. My brother-in-law then got into the taxi to help me. We both then tried pulling my father. They were trying hard to push. But, the sagging door of the taxi was a problem for them. It wouldn't stay steady and would bang against them. The grumpy driver was watching the whole scene, standing at a distance, with an obstinate aloofness, twisting his long, bushy moustache.

The man who was accompanying me felt peeved at it

and so yelled at him, "You, the child of a pig! Can't you just lay your hand on the door of your old, haggard taxi?"

The driver was a *sardarjee*. Pointing his finger at the man, he shouted back in his husky voice, "Hey! You old haggard numbskull! Don't yell at me. Haven't I told you I am not going to touch the dead body?"

The man shouted back furiously, "You bloody whack! Who's asking you to hold the dead body? Hold your bloody, sagging door steady, you rascal!" And, as he was shouting, looking back at the *sardarjee*, the dead body slipped out of his grip, and the lower part of it lay hanging from the seat of the taxi.

Yelling was going on between them, and half of my father's dead body was still hanging from the taxi. Holding his head precariously with my whole body bending over it, I couldn't tolerate the situation anymore, and again like a child, I burst into loud crying, loud enough to stop the brawl. Perhaps my helpless cry softened the *sardarjee* a little. He stopped shouting and came forward to hold the door steady. The dead body was then pushed onto the seat of the taxi, but again a problem arose that there was no space inside for the legs since my father was quite tall, and moreover, because of the inordinate delay, the dead body had become so stiff that in no way could the legs be twisted a bit. The *sardarjee* then graciously advised someone to sit by the side of the dead body holding the door ajar and assured us that he would be driving slowly.

Thus, almost squatting by the side of his dead body, I accompanied my father in his last journey. On the other side was my sister's disgruntled husband with one of his hands pushing the door of the taxi back, silently cursing his dead father-in-law for leaving this earth without fulfilling the assurance of the rest of the dowry. The man, who had been looking after me right from the railway station, in the meantime, had become quite chummy with the *sardarjee*. They were exchanging cigarettes. The overcast sky had cleared up a little, and faint moonlight slantingly fell on my father's face. It was for the first time after his death that I looked at him so intently. I had never looked at him so, even when he was living. Barring childhood days, I don't remember a time when we had talked face to face, looking at each other. By the time I grew up, he had already turned into a depressed figure, sitting or walking or talking with a drooping head, overcome with an obsession of not being able to raise a house of his own, and if you don't have a house of your own, where do you belong? What are you living for?

Looking at his calm face, I wanted to see whether it still wore the obsession. A cloud covered the moon, and it became dark inside. In darkness, I was wondering if my father's soul would rest in peace. Does death bring an end to everything? I was told that if a man dies with a strong desire unfulfilled, his soul suffers a lot. What would happen to my father? Would he still be suffering? What did he live for then, if suffering is the only thing, living or dead? The moon appeared again in the cloudy sky. I looked at my father's face. There was no expression.

Sitting at a distance on a boulder, we saw the pyre in flames. There was no electricity, because of the heavy downpour, and so the electric crematorium was not functioning. In fact, the man accompanying me from the railway station had arranged everything needed for the funeral rites: different varieties of earthen pots, flowers (wilted, of course), new white cloth, puffed rice, ghee, matches, banana leaves (which he collected from the backyard of a nearby house ignoring a barking dog). All these articles were available on the cremation ground. There were shops for these things. Pyre-wood was also available. But, it was wet and so kerosene was to be bought. But, he had a very tough time in arranging a *purohit* without whom the rites could not be performed. I noticed that the man was quite familiar with such situations. He took the taxi, and within minutes, he came back along with a priest who told me bluntly that since it was an unusual time he would charge double the normal amount. It was then that I remembered that I hadn't enough money with me, and in the meantime, I took a glance at the main entrance of the cremation ground and saw that the taxi was not there which meant that the man had already made the payment. I looked at the man with a sense of gratitude, and he assured the priest that he would be paid so. With a broad grin on his face, the priest immediately started reciting mantras even without waiting for the articles to be arranged and placed properly in the appropriate direction. The man didn't bother about it. He let the priest do his work and seated himself on the ground giving his helping hand when asked. I was asked to fetch water from the river in a new earthen pitcher. The dead body was totally uncovered. I poured water from the pitcher on the naked body of my father, and he was properly bathed. And then, I was asked to smear ghee on the whole body. I did so. With the help of the crematorium laborers available on the spot, the dead body was raised and laid on the pyre after going three times around it. Different sizes and shapes of pyre wood were placed in a very scientific way so that the dead body would burn to the last of the bones. And, as per the custom, I had to put the torch on my father's corpse so that the wood would catch the fire, and so I stooped over his face to see for the last time if there was any expression on it. Was he leaving the earth with his desire for the house unfulfilled? It must be very painful, very painful for him. At least, here it was me whom he could confide in. And to whom would he be talking about his pain? It must be very stifling for him. Oh God! Help my father! Help my father! It was not his fault that he had to desert his native place. It was not his fault that his ancestral relationships were all torn apart. It was not his fault that he had to carry along an obsession for a house all through his life. It was not his fault that he turned a refugee. God! Help my father! I raised my hands in prayer. They thought that I was overcome with grief and was about to faint, so the man rushed to me and held me in his arms and led me towards a boulder lying there.

Sitting there at a distance on a boulder, I watched the pyre burning and along with it my father. The silence of the late night increased the hissing of the flames. Again, the black clouds had started collecting in the sky above. The wind too began to be gusty. It was then that suddenly I became curious about the man. He came along with me straight from the station and had not left my company, a complete stranger helping me in all the ways possible. Simply strange!

I turned towards him and asked, "All through this you are with me, and your family, your people, must be worrying. You haven't been to your home nor have you sent any message."

The man smiled and didn't say anything. For the first time since I arrived here, I felt very much concerned about him and told him so without hiding my sense of guilt.

The man was half-lying on the ground. At my expression of concern, he lay straight on his back looking up at the overcast sky and then broke the silence, "My family isn't here staying with me. They are far away in the village."

I said, "I see. You are staying here alone."

"Yes," the man said, "and for years."

"For years! Why? You aren't going to your village?"

The man sighed deeply and said, "No. I'm not going. They don't even come, either. In fact, they can't. They are helpless."

I asked, "Who are they?"

He said, "My wife, my son, and my two daughters."

I was at a loss to understand anything from this talk, and so I just gave a blank look at him. The wind became gusty for a while, and the flames rose high. The man noticed my blank face. He sat up and said, "They have deserted me. Only that I send money every month."

With much hesitation, I asked feebly, "Divorced?"

The man denied it strongly, shaking his head. He got up, and sitting by my side, he said, "It's a story. Almost a story. Years back, I got embroiled in a village dispute. Of course, it was my nature. You can say my habit. I tend to be involved in anything that doesn't necessarily concern my family or me. My wife would sometimes react to it. But, I don't know why I just can't help it. So, it happened once in my village. My village, you know, is in a very remote area. I happen to be the first graduate from there. You see, staying here in town, you cannot imagine the plight of my village. It is still wallowing in the medieval period. Some years back, do you know what happened? The only son of our village priest fell in love with the girl of our village cobbler. The boy, the priest's son, was very bright. On my weekends, when I used to go to the village, I would personally look after his study. The priest, too, also was very happy about the care I showed for his son. It so happened that the boy secured a rank in the school final exam. It was beyond our expectations. The whole village was excited over it, and so I proposed to take him to the town for an admission in a good college here.

"The priest at first didn't agree and said, 'What is the need for further study? My son is a matriculate. That is enough. He should now start learning his family trade. I am growing old. Who would see to your religious needs after my death? Won't it be a shame to invite priests from other villages?'" But, ultimately, he had to yield under the pressure of the villagers, some landlords and the important old people of the village. They convinced him that his son would bring name and fame to our village. But, you see! Things turned in such a way that I found myself in a very delicate situation when one night the boy who was then in the fourth year of his medical study came over to me and confided in me about his love for the cobbler's girl whose marriage was almost fixed, and that if the boy didn't marry her immediately, she was sure to commit suicide.

"'She is a very sensitive girl and highly sentimental, too,' the priest's son told me. The boy was in desperate need of my help. Do you know what I did then?" He looked at me with a beaming face. Naturally, how could I know? He then resumed, "The next morning, I went to my village. I met the girl, confirmed from her what the boy had told me, and that same evening, without making any fuss, without giving any chance for doubt, I brought the girl here and got them married through registration with sincere help from his friends and medical teachers." He stopped and taking a long breath said, "Do you know where they are now? Last year, the boy completed his medical study and immediately he got a scholarship for higher study abroad. He is now in London along with that cobbler's girl, his sensitive, sentimental wife."

There was a deep silence. The sky was overcast with thick clouds. The wind had become gustier. It had started blowing strongly. With the strong wind, the river water had also started overflowing the banks. The cremation ground was on a low level, and the overflowing river water was causing a threat to the burning pyre of my father. The crematory people, looking after the fire of the pyre, told us so. The man asked how long it would take. They simply gestured their ignorance but were very categorical that it would certainly take more than the usual time and then started lecturing us that we should not have allowed the corpse to stay for such a long time. It gets stiff, and it is a very laborious process to burn such a stiffened corpse. They even said that they were still doing it at the normal rate, because they saw that the corpse belonged to that helpless young man. The man encouraged them by promising some more wages, if they could speed up the process and finish the work before the rising water reached the pyre and wash it away. They looked satisfied at this and showed more enthusiasm.

It seemed that daybreak was not far off. The man, sitting by my side, was looking at the rising river. I asked him, "Is it for this that your family has deserted you?"

The man said calmly, "No, it is not for that my family has abandoned me. Two days after the marriage was over, I went to my village to tell them everything and to try to persuade them to accept it. But, when I reached my village, I was stunned to see my house burnt down completely. My wife, my son, and my daughters, I saw sitting blankly under the mango trees in the backyard surrounded by a host of curious villagers, mostly women and children. In the midst of the smoke and the smell of the burnt bamboo, I stood there helplessly. Immediately, I decided that I would bring them all here at my workplace. I also learnt that the *panchayat* of the village had decided last evening that my whole family had been ostracised. We could not use the village well. My children would not be allowed to be in the school. We could not participate in any of the community functions nor the villagers in our functions. Even the village temple was forbidden to us. When I tried to persuade my wife to leave the village, she stubbornly refused.

"She persistently said, "How can I live with grown up daughters among the strangers there? Have I ever gone out of the village even for a single day? How can you live with people whom you don't know? They are not even your relations? How can you live in a strange place?' She went on asking. And, when I asked her how she could leave her own village after marrying me, she innocently said, "But then, this is not a strange place for me? It is your village. You were born here, and you belong to this place, and so I also belong to this place. How am I to abandon my place now and move on like a destitute?' In the evening, her father came and through his mediation a compromise was made with the village chiefs that my family would be allowed to stay, on the condition that all the members of my family including my little youngest daughter would apologise in front of the whole village and that I, the main culprit, would never touch the boundary of the village. Neither could the members of my family be in touch with me for as long as I lived. The last condition was that when I die, my dead body would not be brought to the village, nor would my son give fire to my face."

"Your wife accepted it all?"

The man kept mum. I thought he couldn't hear, and so I repeated the question. "Your wife accepted it all?"

Still there was silence. After a long time the man spoke, "Don't know whether she accepted it or not, but she says she has been fated so and that she is a cursed woman."

Again, silence reigned. I wanted to know if he had any remorse for what he had done. The man laughed and said, "Yes, sometimes. Sometimes I regret. After all, who would like to be self-exiled?" The man took a pause and then resumed, "But, you know I am like that. That is my nature. And now, one thing is happening to me. I am getting involved in more and more social activities, and so I'm not left with much time for brooding." He stopped, and then suddenly, he sprang up and looking straight at me asked, "Now, you see, had I not offered my help what could you have done? You would have simply allowed your father to rot and stink there in the hospital corridor. And by the by, I also see that you don't have money too with you."

At these words, I suddenly remembered the piece of paper my co-passenger in the train had given to me. I told him so and brought the letter out of my pocket and said, "Here is the address." The man tried to read the address. The wind blew strongly, and in the rising flame of the pyre, he glimpsed it, and then giving me the description of a man, he asked excitedly, "Is it this type of a man who gave you this address?"

I said, "Yes."

The man then grimaced and shouted: "That bloody bastard! This son of a bitch was instrumental in uprooting me from my village. And, do you know why has he given this letter to you? To mock me. To torture me. That bastard is still under the illusion that I have left all my social work. And that I must be wallowing in misery, in remorse, in desperation." The man stopped and laughed.

The crematory people suddenly gave an alarming cry: "Oh! Sirs! The water has started reaching the pyre!" We both looked back. We were so engrossed in our talk that we had not noticed how the level of the water had been rising fast. We saw in amazement the flowing water all over the cremation ground. I started trembling in anxiety and fear when I could see clearly how the wooden pyre was wobbling at the strike of the strong current of the floodwater. The darkness was slowly disappearing in the eastern sky. A faint brightness was reflected in the madding waves of the rising river-water. I felt appalled at the sight. At any moment, it was going to swallow up the half-burnt body of my father! And, if it so happened, what would be the fate of my father's soul! Would it be more painful for him? Oh God! My shivering palm gripped the hand of the man so violently that he, too, got scared. And, before any of us could do or think anything, a strong stormy wind with huge raindrops and a deafening thunder with a blinding lightning shook us thoroughly. Our eyes closed.

When I opened my eyes, I helplessly watched as my father was washed away into the river. The current was so strong that within moments, his half-burnt floating body was immersed in the dark blue water of the river.

I stood still in the enormity of the blankness. No father. No trace of him.

Two

"My Love is like a red, red rose"

Long back, when I was in my early youth, I had written this line on a crumpled, soiled paper. Purposelessly. It was not meant for anybody, nor did I have any feeling of love then or anything of that sort. I was sitting on the outer veranda of my friend's house in a remote village. Our friendship had developed suddenly and in a very strange way. He was my classmate. Once, while coming from the college, he offered me a lift on his bicycle and on the way asked which village I had come from.

I said, "No village."

He laughed and said, "Oh! You're a pure *sahari* (town-bred)?"

I said, "No, not even that."

He said "Then what? Neither village-bred nor town-bred, falling straight from the heaven?"

I said, "Ha, something like that. Not exactly falling but floating. As the story of my birth goes, I was born on the wooden planks of a boat floating on a river." At my playfulness, he burst into such a boisterous laughter that he lost his balance, and we both fell down on the road. Even lying on the road with the bicycle on him, he went on laughing.

When he rose to his feet, he hugged me intimately and said, "You are really very interesting!" and that was how we started our friendship. Later, it became that every holiday he would invite me to his village, and I would be happy enough to accompany him.

The first time I went with him was in a summer. My

friend's village was in a remote area, miles away from the railway station. Even if you go by bus, his village remains far away from the bus stop. In fact, truly speaking, it was neither a bus stop nor a railway station. Half an hour before the bus reaches that stop, the conductor in the bus would start shouting, "Is there anybody there to get down here?" And, you would have to stand at the door of the bus ready to get down the moment the bus slowed down there. It wouldn't stop, unless of course, there were passengers to get in or the passenger was a woman or extremely old. The railway station was also no different. It was just a passenger halt. The train would halt but only for seconds. You were to literally jump down. That was what we did. I had no idea about it. As the train started slowing down, my friend caught hold of the rod of the door and asked me to do so, and the moment the train came to a halt he bumped himself down onto the platform and so did I without knowing what it was for. But, I saw that by the time we stood up the train had already left the small platform. So, I came to know what it was for.

The platform was so small that it took no time to cross over. At the end of it, there was a huge, tall, shady *peepal* tree, and under the tree was a small cabin for tea. It was early morning. I saw the tea kettle on the red burning firewood, and we had tea there. The place was so quiet, open, and sprawling that I liked it very much. The vast stretch of open land cast its own charm on me. I told my friend that I would love to come to his village frequently. He felt glad and said, "Do come. I don't have real friends here."

We walked down on the ridges of the parched paddy fields. There was no rainfall for a long time, and the soil had dried up exposing the cracked furrows. We didn't have any difficulty in walking on the ridges. My friend explained that there was no other communication to his village. People get down from the bus or the train and then start walking. Of course, during the rainy seasons, it would be certainly very inconvenient.

Walking down from the station to my friend's house

was really an experience for me. I had no intimate knowledge of a village. The only knowledge that I had till that day was more or less fictional in the story of my birth as told by my mother. But, the landscape in that story was completely different. In fact, there was not much scope for the description of the landscape, and if it was there, it was mainly of rivers or coconut trees, nothing else. As I was walking along with my friend, the atmosphere looked so fresh, pleasant, and wonderful: a clear blue sky and bright sunshine sprawling over our heads; intimate nature, open and stretching all around us; trees, sometimes standing lonely and sometimes densely in a grove; birds, sitting or chirping visibly or invisibly behind the leaves of the trees; sometimes the rustling of leaves as the birds would fly up at the sound of our footsteps; birds flying alone or in a flock against the blue sky; cows grazing on the field, unconcerned; acquaintances and fellow villagers on the way; if older persons, my friend wishing them *Namaskar* and the old man asking since it's not Sunday today, why he was back home and my friend replying that it's a long vacation; the old man then asking the meaning of vacation and my friend explaining that the college is closed at which the old man would call the college authority cheats since they take money and close the college sending us back home and that God will not tolerate such ungodly acts.

Suddenly, the old man would stop on the way, taking a sad look at the parched field lying before him and would make a kind of monologue, "It's not for nothing that the mother earth is lying on her back with the gaping mouth looking up thirstily for a drop of rain! It's already midsummer, and there is yet no sign of a silver line in the sky! It's because of these ungodly acts! Ungodly acts!"

By the time we reached my friend's house, the sun had already gone up in the sky. We reached his house from the backside of the village. We had to go round on the uneven bank of a small pond to enter the backyard of the house where I saw a girl drawing water from the well. Seeing us, she smiled at my friend and greeted him as her elder brother, saying: "How come the untimely cloud today?" meaning thereby how was my friend seen there although it was not a holiday? My friend replied with a mischievous smile that he had come on a surprise visit to check if the lazy girl of the village was doing her chores, and then asked her to come to the kitchen and make some tea for us. My friend then led me into his house. We entered into a wide courtyard, divided into two parts, the lower part down below with two small rooms, kitchen, and storeroom, the upper part, raised a bit from the ground with two steps, having a row of two or three rooms. In the middle of the courtyard, a *tulsi* plant on a small platform made of earth, smeared with cow-dung and water, looking neat and fresh in the sunshine. To its left was a small hut-like room with a low thatched roof about a man's height, the room for the family gods. We had to cross them all to go up to the upper part. As I was led through one corner room connected to the main entrance of the house, there was a typical pungent smell, and the room was quite dark, too. As I entered, in the faint sunlight coming through the door, I could see that it was the cowshed. We came out onto the outer veranda. There was bright sunshine. My friend asked me to sit on the mat that was spread on the veranda. I sat there and saw some slender books and notebooks scattered over the mat. My friend said that perhaps his sister and that girl were in study there.

"Who?" I asked. "That lazy girl of the village you saw?" Asking me to take a rest, my friend then went inside the house.

I was sitting on the veranda alone. There were some tall coconut trees just in front of it. The veranda and its adjacent ground looked chequered with sunlight falling through the long ripped leaves of the coconut trees. It was there while sitting quietly and enjoying the still freshness of a village morning that my eyes fell on the neighbouring, small, cozy garden. It was typically a garden of roses, all red, a lot of them. The sudden sight of a number of blood-red roses at the time fascinated and pleased me immensely. I had never seen such red roses in such a number. Looking at it, a line from a poem I had read somewhere came to my mind, and unconsciously, I took a notebook and pencil lying there and wrote down on its crumpled paper, "My love is like a red, red rose."

I had never given a thought even in my wildest imagination that a line from a poem on a piece of crumpled paper, one day, would wreck the life of an innocent girl, my loved one, from within.

My visits to my friend's village then became so frequent that the neighbours of my friend started to look upon me almost as a member of his family. Even once, I had been there alone. My friend had stayed back for some work in the town and joined me there in his village the next day. No one seemed to have been surprised at this. The curiosity about me was there, of course, but it was mainly in the early days. Once that curiosity was over, nobody took notice of my visit. It became almost as natural as my friend going to his own village, his own home. In the process, I developed a friendship and intimacy with many people there, mostly of my age. My growing intimacy with that girl, the lazy girl of the village as my friend used to tease her, was perhaps a part of this process. And, it started the very first day of my visit when, while sipping tea, I was appreciating the rose garden of my friend's neighbour. My friend was highly pleased with my appreciation and asked me, "Want to go there?" Immediately, he stood up and said, "Let's go. She would be very happy."

"Who?" I asked out of ignorance.

My friend said, "That girl, the lazy girl of the village. It's her garden to tell you the truth. Her father doesn't like it. He is totally opposed to it. In fact, her father had prepared the soil for growing vegetables. He had sown the seeds also, but the next day it was seen that all those seeds had been raked up and thrown away. Her father got angry, and she was beaten up when she admitted that she had committed the mischief. But, the girl was so obstinate she didn't allow any vegetable seeds to be sown there. 'What do you want then?' the father one day asked her irritatingly. 'I want to raise a flower garden there,' the girl said in tears."

"And then, her father agreed?" I asked.

My village friend said, "Not exactly agreed, rather gave in. She is his only child naa, and he just can't ignore her wish. But, he made it clear that he was not going to help her in any way. It was up to her to grow the flower plants."

"And she did it alone?" I asked. My friend nodded his head. "Wonderful!" I said.

And, it was still to be seen how "wonderful" she herself looked in the garden in the closeness of those plants and flowers, when we went there. In fact, it was her father who came out seeing us in the garden. My friend introduced me to him and said all about my appreciation for the plants and flowers. Her father made a wry face and went in and perhaps told his daughter, for the next moment, we saw the girl rushing down to the garden. She stopped there, gasping, looking at us without words, with a smile spread all over her tender face and a pair of dark eloquent eyes liquidly filled with a sense of gratitude. She stood there, still, shining like a blossom in the bright sunlight. She looked so fresh, so tender, so innocent, and so wonderful!

A note of wonder was there in her, perhaps. It wasn't until months later that I started realising how strongly she had struck at the very core of my emotions. Back home, in the beginning days of my romance with her, it was the typical scene of a girl drawing water from the well and smiling at us that haunted me for a long time. In my lonely hours, the very recollection of the scene would let pass waves of pleasing sensations through my whole body and that would ultimately end up with painful throbs. I used to reason it out as the natural expression of my subdued obsession for a homely, intimate village life. The obsession had a strange origin. Once, while moving in a bus, a typical sight attracted me very much. I didn't know why. It was by the side of a village. The bus halted there for a long time because of some mechanical snag. Just on the other side of the road was the backyard of a house, and there was a well and I noticed a whole village life around that well. A young girl was drawing water from the well while an elderly woman stood in wait with a number of pots of different sizes to be filled by the girl. When filled, the old woman was carrying them into the house. An elderly man under a tree nearby was telling them something in a monotonous tone while busy mending a fishing net. Another one was participating in the talk while pouring water over his head on this side of the well. Even the girl drawing water from the well joined in either through some gestures or nods or with crisp comments, and then a naked child with a protruding stomach appeared there, crying full-throated and complaining against her mother, and the girl drawing water from the well consoled the child with let her work be over and she would see to it. All these details around a well had impressed me terribly that day, and it got sunk so deep into my subconscious that the scene of a well at the backyard of a house anywhere I came across would attract me passionately.

So, it happened in the case of that girl, too. Even today, I am not clear about what it was exactly that made me fall in love with her, the lazy girl of the village, as my friend used to call her. Was it the scene at the well pulsating in me an obsessed sensation of a village intimacy? Or, the sublime scene at the rose garden where one could hardly differentiate the wonder of the garden from that of the gardener? I do not know what it was.

The only thing that used to worry me was that coming back home from my friend's village, each time, I would feel restless, and my restlessness would go on mounting as I would be waiting for the next vacation to come, or even holidays for a short duration when my friend would ask me to accompany him to his village. With such frequent visits, the intimacy between us grew so immensely that neither of us, neither she nor me nor even anybody else in their families, had ever noticed that there was a marked change in her behaviour with me in the meantime from the coyness of a village girl to the casualness of a family member. It meant that we used to talk intimately, freely, and alone, and no one would take notice of it or even look upon it as unusual.

One evening, sitting on a mat in the inner courtyard of my friend's house, I was explaining to them, my friend's sister and that lazy girl, certain rudimentary things about the simple sentence in English, which had become a usual phenomenon during my stay there, when my friend's sister went away to help her mother in the kitchen. The girl then, taking a wary look around her, brought out from inside her frock a crumpled sheet of paper and placing it before me asked in a hushed tone, "What is its meaning?" I picked up the paper and flicking through it started laughing loudly at which the girl suddenly punching me hard on my stretched thigh made signs to me to be quiet, taking a startling look at the kitchen.

I failed to understand what was secretive about it. But, anyway, I told her that it was a line from an English poem I had read somewhere and that it came to my mind when I happened to see her rose garden and also that the whole thing happened spontaneously. She asked me, in the same hushed tone, "What does it mean?" I explained the meaning of it in her own language - that it was a kind of finding a similarity between the feeling of love and that of a red-coloured rose. I also tried to point out the significance of the colour red implying passion, and then I realised that all these were meaningless since she was not perhaps of age to understand all those intricacies either of love or of poetry, when I noticed that instead of trying to follow what I was saying, she was simply looking at me abstractly. So, I stopped, and the moment I stopped, she almost threw a question at me, "Why did you write all these things in my notebook?" I was trying to explain to her that I had not written all those things; in fact, I had simply casually quoted a line when she saw my friend's sister coming out of the kitchen at which I didn't know why she immediately put that piece of crumpled paper back inside her frock and ran away almost brushing against her friend. My friend's sister looked at me questioningly. I shrugged off and said, "Might be she had forgotten something she was asked to do by her parents."

She laughed and said, "Haa, that's very much her habit."

The matter did not end there. The whole scene went on haunting me, for I began to mark that after that incident she had been behaving with me in a strange and awkward manner that went almost unnoticed by others. The very casualness in her dealings was gradually dying away. I marked particularly that she was avoiding being alone with me. And, if at all left alone, she would keep quiet, unless I asked her something and then too evading a straight look at me. Sometimes, it so happened that sitting along with others, if I put more attention to the others, to my friend's sister in particular, she would sulk and would leave the place silently.

It pained me very much. I liked the girl who had looked so jolly and cheerful, always bubbling with animated buoyancy. Her changed countenance, therefore, disturbed me terribly. One evening, an interesting thing happened. Some children, her friends and those friends' little brothers and their friends, surrounded me. The attraction was the jokes I was telling. I used to tell jokes and that might have spread widely and so the gathering. What surprised and pleased me was that the lazy girl was back to her former demeanor, laughing and rolling down on the mat with as much excitement as shown by others. In the middle of my joke-session, suddenly, the sound of a party band and that of fireworks was heard, and instantly all the children, ignoring my presence, rushed to the door and ran away with shouts of joy. The lazy girl was also running away along with them, shouting cheerfully when I made her stop and asked for a glass of water. The girl ran inside and in no time fetched a glass of water. Placing the glass on the floor, she was about to make for the door when I asked her to stay back. She turned round and glancing at me for a fleeting moment, stooped her face down and suddenly became sullen.

Standing at the door, I said, "I have something to ask you." She stood there, unmoved, for a while, and then suddenly, throwing a mysterious look at me, ran away almost as if for her life, leaving me still more confounded.

In fact, I wanted to know what exactly it was that had changed her behaviour towards me. Sitting there alone in the room, I was brooding over the possible reasons. Wondering if ever I had unknowingly hurt her sentiments, my friend entered the room. He slumped himself on the bare floor by my side and looked distracted. I said, "Hey, where have you been, leaving me alone here?"

My friend turned to me and giving the same distracted look said, "I told you I was going to see my uncle, Aunty wasn't well."

I nodded my head, "*Han haan*, you said something like that. How is she now? What's the problem with her? Was it something serious?" I went on asking. Getting no response, I got anxious, "You stayed there for a long time. Where is she now? In the hospital?"

This time my friend responded, shrugging, "No, she is alright, in her own house. Nothing has happened. It was only that my uncle got a bit scared."

"About?" I asked.

My friend said, "About my aunt. She was like that for a long time. It used to happen to her occasionally, once a while. But, as my uncle says it has now become a regular feature with her and that worries him."

"But, what is it exactly? What's the problem with your aunt?" I asked.

My friend remained silent and took a long time to reply, "The problem is obvious, at least to me and to my uncle, but the very appearance of that problem is quite puzzling, disturbing also." The tone and the reclining position that he took against the wall clearly suggested that he was going to tell me the story of his uncle and aunt about which he had given me some hints months before I had learnt that she was having some psychological problems. When I asked what kind of problem, he said that she was getting scared towards the evening in particular, and that sometimes standing at the window that looks out to the open backyard, she would send such chilling shouts in her shrill voice that it would even set her neighbours to panic. Often, it so happened that her neighbors would rush to their house and would be surprised that everything was normal there. Rather, it was his aunt who would ask them in astonishment, "What happened?"

I knew that my friend was going to tell me more about this. So, I remained silent. My friend started on his own, "It is nothing but a sense of guilt that is working in her." My friend said this almost as a monologue and stopped. I looked at him with a silent question. He replied on his own, "Yes, it's the guilt of infanticide." I was surprised, infanticide! My friend said, "Yes, they are having four children now, and all of them are daughters. Every year after their marriage, she used to bear a child, and after the fourth child, my uncle advised her to have an abortion, and then every year, she would undergo abortion almost routinely even against her will, resulting in her failing health and constant insomnia. When she would tell about her health problems, my uncle would simply laugh it away advising her rather to take more milk which was there in plenty in his own house. In fact, it was just last year that the situation took a serious turn when the drug that they used to get from a village quack for abortion didn't work properly. My uncle blamed the quack and said, 'The rascal has cheated us!' But, my aunt said that the quack was not to be blamed. This time, the quack had rudely warned against abortion, because he thought it was too late. 'We went to him when I was already in an advanced stage, and it was because we had no inkling of it. There was no sign of pregnancy, and by the time I came to apprehend, it was too late, and so the quack was reluctant,' said my aunt. But, my uncle, as I learned, was insistent, and so ultimately, the quack gave in but with a warning that it might turn out to be dangerous for both the child and the mother."

My friend said, "Do you know what my uncle did? He collected the drug from the quack throwing in some more money and saying, 'Yes, I know you people very well. These are the tricks you people apply to extract more money. No?'"

I asked, "So, your aunt gave birth to another child? Because, as you said, it didn't work?"

My friend said, "Yes, she did, and that was the tragedy."

"Why tragedy?" I asked.

My friend said, "First of all, because it was a son, and then because it was a stillborn baby. They were awestruck at the sight of a son after four daughters, but the very sight of a cold, lifeless baby tore their hearts apart."

I said, "I understand. They must have been filled with remorse that had they tried to get it aborted. Perhaps the baby-son could have been saved!"

My friend nodded his head and said, "No, not exactly. The tragedy started much later, ensuing from what happened to the stillborn."

"What happened to the baby?" I asked.

My friend said, "My uncle asked the village *ayah* attending to her to take the stillborn and bury it somewhere outside the village. It was already evening and was raining as well. The *ayah* was reluctant, but when my aunt entreated her to be merciful, she agreed, wrapped the baby in a bed sheet, and went out in the darkness of the evening with a grumpy face. The next morning, before the daybreak, my aunt suddenly woke up from her sleep at the raucous howling of some curs outside her window at their backyard. She felt too weak to get up from the bed. She could only raise her head and saw some dogs snarling at each other while trying to snatch away something lying on the ground. The sight was not clearly visible. With much difficulty, she raised her head a little more, and in the foggy atmosphere, she saw a dog running away with something in its mouth which looked hazily like that of her baby and other dogs snarling and chasing it."

"Horrible! Horrible! It makes my hair stand!" I said.

My friend said, "So, you imagine the impact of the sight on my aunt! Maddening! She could never come round from that terrible shock in her life. And, that is why she would behave like that when she would look out through that window, sending a heart-piercing cry in her shrill voice at the sight of her stillborn bitten into pieces by snarling curs, as though she could see it even years after!"

What to speak of my friend's aunt, back home, day after day the sight of a baby slinging from between the sharp teeth of a dog being chased by a host of snarling dogs stayed stuck before my eyes. The moment I would be alone or lying on my bed in the lonely room, the scene would appear before my eyes, gnawing, and my whole body would start shuddering, an unknown ambiguous pain would make those moments unbearable for me. The following week, in fact, I could not sleep. For whole nights, I would stay awake, feeling restive.

It was this shocking scene of a baby slinging from between the sharp teeth of a dog that ultimately wrecked my loved one's life. In fact, since the day my friend told me about his uncle and aunt, I had not been to his village for a long time. Somehow or other, I was overcome with a vague sense of suffering. All the while, I would feel as though a lump of pain had got stuck inside my heart, and I was neither able to remove it nor even able to speak about it before anyone. It was possibly a kind of depression that I was undergoing, and so I was rather avoiding my friend.

Months after, during a vacation, I went to my friend's village alone. When I reached his village, it was almost evening. The sun had set, but the darkness of the night was yet to engulf the village. Reaching his house, I was struck by an unusual hushed atmosphere. I pushed the entrance door but was surprised that the door which used to remain open till the midnight sleeping time did not open even at my push. I was at a loss to understand the whole situation. Just as I was looking around to ask someone I happened to come across, I was startled by a peal of subdued laughter. Stepping down the steps, I saw her, the lazy girl of the village, behind me with a bunch of keys in her palm.

I asked, "What's the matter? Where are they?" She didn't give any reply. Placing her hand with the keys behind, she swayed and smiled at me with an air of playful enchantment. I again asked, "What's the matter? Where are they?" This time also she repeated her swaying motion and a mysterious smile. She really looked funny. So, I said teasingly, "See, you really look so pretty in your swaying motion, but would you be pleased enough to answer me where are they?" at which she suddenly became serious.

The smile disappeared from her face, and she asked me sullenly, "What if they are not there? Can't I look after you?" Pulling on her face, she went to the door, unlocked it, pushed it open, and went inside. I followed her. She stood there silently for some time and then said, "Your meals would be arranged, don't worry," threw away the keys in my face and was going away sulkily, when I caught hold of her hands. She stopped, didn't try to get rid of my hold, and looked at me with a strange expression in her eyes. I was drawn by her deep black eyes with a magnetic charm in them. I was surprised that I had never discovered it before. She let her whole body rest on me, her tender breasts touching my body softly. A strange warm sensation flowed through me downwards. I felt tempted. I held her tightly. She, too, held me tightly, at which I could feel the erection. I gave a clumsy kiss on her cheek. She started rubbing her cheeks on my whole face. My hands fumbled passionately on her back, at which she started feeling restless. She held my hand and placed it on her small round breast, pressing her nipple. I squeezed it, and she got terribly excited. I felt scared that my friend's family might get in anytime, and so I asked about them again.

She embraced me violently, pressing her soft body against me madly and said, gasping, "No, no, they aren't coming back so soon. Aunty has expired."

I was literally taken aback, letting her out of my hold. But, she drew me towards her as she was lying down on the floor. I was still standing there, stupefied, when she unbuttoned her frock exposing a pair of small lovely breasts with reddish nipples like rose buds glaring at me. I could not resist myself. Our two warm naked bodies holding each other intimately, tightly, passionately, rolling over each other on the bare floor, reached a state of irresistibly pleasing sensation. Hotly aroused, I was about to penetrate her soft wetness, the intermittent touching of which aroused an uncontrollable passion in her, too, when suddenly, the sight of that baby in the mouth of a dog appeared before my eyes. I had just pushed the tip of my erection into her when I vividly visualised that horrendous scene, and instantly all my passions froze. My whole sexual caressing suddenly stopped. I could helplessly feel my erection was shrinking and shrinking. My whole body became cold. I could not feel. There was no sensation. It was deadened. A deadened naked body was lying on her. I saw, she was looking at me imploringly, blankly, strangely, failing to grasp what went wrong. The suddenness of the development also rendered her speechless. She lay there absolutely stupefied for a while, and then suddenly, she stood up, picked up her frock, put it on, and to my utter shame and surprise, with a spiteful utterance of "thooh! thooh! thooh!" she spat on me three times and ran away.

I was sitting there, alone, in the darkness, feeling the warm lump of phlegm on my face, head and shoulder. I did not try to wipe it off.

I felt terribly upset not so much by my sexual misadventure as by the visualisation of that hair-raising sight of a dead human baby bitten into pieces by a pack of motley mutts.

It was almost a year after that incident I went to my friend's village again. In the meantime, I tried to put my desire to marry that girl across my friend's mind. But, either I didn't get an opportunity to raise the topic, or even though I had given hints of it, he couldn't get at it. Also, by that time, since our studies were over, we used to meet each other less frequently, when my friend would come over to the town in connection with some work in the hospital or in any office or for jobs. If he could take time off his work, he would come straight to my place. I was also then looking for a job. And, that was the reason I could not gather courage to propose.

It was during this period that one day my friend asked if I was coming to his village next month to attend the wedding ceremony.

I felt delighted and said, "Sure, your sister is marrying and I won't come? What do you think of me?"

We were talking at the bus stop waiting for the bus to his village, and my friend said, "No, not exactly my own sister."

"Who is it then?" I asked.

My friend said, "That lazy girl you know, your rose-garden girl. Her marriage has been fixed for the next month." And, just then, the bus came, and my friend tried to get into the overcrowded bus elbowing others as far as possible. Before I had the time to ask him anything more, the bus started to move.

The very next morning, my friend was surprised to see me in his village, "Are! You didn't tell me yesterday that you would be coming!"

I said, "No, in fact..." I fumbled for words and then said, "In fact, after you came back, I thought I hadn't come to your village for a long time, and so I thought I had better go today, and so I came." I tried to laugh.

My friend was extremely delighted for he said that he was also getting bored without a friend there. And then suddenly he proposed: "Let's go fishing."

"Fishing? Where?"

My friend said, "Just a couple of miles from our village, there is a river. I used to go there long back. Let's go. You would really enjoy it." As he was saying this, my eyes were roving round for a glimpse of the lazy girl. I was not interested in what he was saying nor did I want to leave his house even for a moment without talking to that girl. But strangely, she was not to be seen anywhere around, even though I was deliberately talking in an unusually loud voice. In the meantime, my friend's sister came with tea and puffed rice.

I asked her jokingly, "Coming alone! Seems your friend has deserted you even long before the marriage!"

She smiled and said, "No, she was here with me but went away. Told me that she had a lot of work at home."

At this, I felt depressed. I could realise that she was trying to avoid me. Nobody knew why. Only I could guess. And, it upset me terribly. I felt restless to know what exactly was on her mind. All the while as we were sitting there in the front veranda, I was frantically looking for her to talk to her. But, she was nowhere. As a matter of fact, I had been to her village with an absurd thought that if I could get a chance to talk to her alone, I was sure, she would definitely agree to marry me, and in that case, I would try to convince her father, too.

The thought was definitely absurd. But, that is what I come to realise now. The absurdity part of it, I mean. For me, it was then a thrilling proposition. As all through then, I was toying with that proposition, while talking with my friend or with his sister, a romantic sensation of pleasure was rushing through my whole body I spent the whole morning and noon seeped in that pleasant sensation. But then, as the sunshine of the noon hour started waning with the sun tilting to the west behind the ripped leaves of the coconut trees, I felt I was slowly coming under the grip of a queer pain, an unspeakable, indistinct, unbearable emotion stifling within. It was then that I heard the sound of footsteps in the neighboring rose-garden and at which my heart started pounding heavily.

I had no doubt that it was she, that lazy girl, and I could also guess that she must be looking for me. A hope beamed in me that we could sort out the problem that had become a tangled one due a great extent to my long silence and to some extent by the fixation of her marriage. I was still under a stupid impression that once she was assured of my decision to marry her, she would certainly wriggle out of the tangle by declining the marriage fixed by her parents. I knew she had the guts.

The late noon-hour in the village wore its usual air of silence and solitude. I saw my friend in deep sleep, snoring, after a sumptuous noon-meal. I stood up, and with a throbbing heart, stepped down from the veranda. And, a sensation ran through me when I saw her staring at me and coming forward towards the fence.

I felt extremely delighted and so moved closer towards the fence of hedge, and it was then that it happened. She came straight towards me. Standing on the other side of the shrubby fence, she fixed her steely eyes on me for a minute or so, and then for three times uttering "thooh! thooh! thooh!" she noisily spat on me three times and immediately ran away into her house.

When my friend woke up from his siesta, he saw me

packing up my bag. He asked in surprise, "Hey! What happened? Where are you going?"

I picked up the bag and said, "*Arre*, I suddenly remembered that I have got to attend an interview tomorrow. I had totally forgotten." My friend did not believe it. He was still looking at me in surprise as I started walking down with the bag in my hand.

That was my last visit to his village. That was also my last glimpse of her. I saw her years after when her dead body was brought out of the post-mortem room.

The day before, I happened to come across my friend in our town. He was in a hurry and looked terribly disturbed and distressed. Before I could ask him anything, he straightaway asked me if I knew anybody in the local police station. Before I could ask why, on his own he said, "I will tell you everything later. Now, you first tell me if you could help us." Naturally I hesitated for a moment. Fearing it to be some criminal case, I didn't want to get myself involved in it. My friend noticed my hesitation. He held my hands and implored in a helpless tone: "Please do something. They aren't releasing the dead body. They are yet to get a nod from the police. Delaying any more means it would start stinking." I was taken in by his helplessness. Without trying to enquire any further, I took him straight to a police sub-inspector who once was our neighbour before he moved to his quarters. He used to like me very much, almost like his own son.

It was on the way to the police station that my friend said, "Unfortunate…unfortunate...it's…the whole thing is so unfortunate…it's that girl…that lazy girl, you know."

I was shocked, "What happened to her?"

My friend said, "It's she…she died."

Perhaps I turned deaf then. I could not hear anything that my friend was telling me. In a stunning silence, we walked down to the police station.

On our way to the cremation ground, I asked my friend, "How did it happen?"

My friend was surprised and said, "That's what I have been telling you since then, on our way to the police station!"

I fumbled, "*Hnaa*...you told...but...I mean...why did she commit suicide?"

At this, my friend expressed utter surprise, "Who told you it was a suicide!"

It took time for me to realise what I was saying. After a long silence, I said, "You see, death at such a tender age...you can't simply explain it."

My friend said, "It happened so suddenly! She was all right even a couple of days before. There was a festival that day of the young girls, and she had come from her in-law's house. She was there with her friends in our house celebrating the festival till late evening when she went away saying that she was not feeling well. The next morning when I saw her she looked quite fresh. It was around the noontime that we could suddenly hear her mother shouting in an alarming tone. When we rushed to her house, we saw her wriggling in pain, gasping for breath. I immediately ran to the local health centre. The doctor, a young man of our own village, examined her but expressed his helplessness and advised us to shift her immediately to the medical hospital. But, on the way, she died. The trouble is that she was carrying, too, so the hospital authority registered it as a police case."

After a long pause my friend said, "In a way, she is responsible for her own death. Her husband was telling me some months back, something like in a complaining tone, that she was an extremely obstinate girl, wouldn't listen to anything, even for her own life." I looked at my friend questioningly, but didn't ask anything. My friend said, "It was about having children. She already had two kids, within three years, a boy and a girl. Her husband, you know, a gentle, considerate, educated young man, wanted to go in for family planning from the very beginning, because, you know, she was of a very tender age. But strangely, she had been vehemently resisting her husband. As her husband used to tell me only in this matter in particular, otherwise, as per her husband, she was an extremely lovely girl, highly sociable, getting along well with everybody in the family, full of respect and affection, sensitive to others' problem." My friend stopped, and then said with a sigh, "God knows why she turned defiant in such a matter! Such a lovely girl! My little sister! And, God wanted her to die at such a tender age!" With tears full in his eyes, he started wailing at the top of his voice as the dead body was lifted onto the pyre.

In stunning silence, I saw a swollen, distorted, stinking corpse slowly engulfed in a consuming fire.

I told to myself that it was a suicide, a slow, deliberate suicide. The helpless expression of a passionate love and a strong hatred for life. For me.

My love died, leaving me alone to suffer.

Three

For a long time, perhaps for a year or so, I slumped into a state of complete indolence. It started when all of a sudden I got a handsome job. I felt so delighted that I couldn't decide what to do with my new self. The job was so attractive that it was beyond my expectation. I was not used to looking upon myself as a person with any potential. It was a kind of discovery, a great discovery of my own self, hitherto lying hidden even to me. My mother heaved a sigh and felt relieved of the impending financial trouble that we were getting to face after the death of my father. My mother said, "It is a timely blessing from God."

In the beginning, I also took it as a blessing. But, as the days went by, and coming face to face with the realities of the pressure of work, a queer sense of apathy started developing in me. If at the headquarters, I would come back from my office in the late evening, and if on tour, it would take some days to get back home. In fact, it was not exactly my home. I was staying alone there at the place of my job in a rented house. And so, naturally, I had no attraction for my home there. In the beginning, I used to go out at 10 o'clock. That was the office time and would come back only after having my dinner in a restaurant on the way. I was a late-riser, too. So, there was no time for me to be at home. The result was that I was slowly losing interest in life, in everything around me. Realising it, I would sit at my table on late nights to carry on the writing of my book The House at Hill-Beauty, but it so happened that I could not write even one complete sentence. Maybe it was due to physical exhaustion. So, over the next few weeks I tried writing on Sundays and holidays but failed. Nothing would come to the tip of my pen. I felt that my mind had gone dry. The creative impulse in me had been dead. It was this awareness that my creativity was lost, had dried up, that haunted me terribly. The more I thought of it, the more I was seized with despair.

It was during this period of my depression that something interesting started happening to me. The house I was staying in also had another portion where a young couple used to stay. They had a little kid, a cute child. I hadn't noticed him. Sometimes in the morning or in the night, I had heard a child crying, or sometimes on my way to the office or back home, I might have passed by the child in the company of his mother or father but had never given any particular attention. It was on one holiday while I was reclining in a chair in my room brooding over my state of inanity that I saw two eyes peeping through the door standing ajar. I tilted my head slightly to have a clear view when suddenly the eyes disappeared, and I could hear the sound of a child running away. I ignored it and took up a book for reading when again I heard a clumsy sound at the door. As I looked up, I saw the same scene of peeping eyes, but this time a part of a child's body was visible. I put the book on the table and looked straight towards the door when again the eyes disappeared, and this time the sound of thudding footsteps was quite faster. I knew that it was my neighbour's little kid.

I smiled to myself, and surprisingly, I felt an urge to have a cup of hot tea. Surprising, because though I had some arrangements for making tea there at my house, I had hardly ever gone for it, if it was not essentially teatime. The urge that I felt then had never happened to me during those days of my depression. So, I went straight into the kitchen and made a nice cup of tea with utmost care. As I was coming back to the drawing room with that cup in my hand, suddenly I heard a bang on the door and a giggle. I put the cup on the table and made for the door.

This time also I could hear the fast fading sound of a child running away, but when I fully opened the door, I saw the cute child holding their door with a part of his body behind the panel of the door. I looked at him and smiled. The child, too, smiled at me exposing a few of his pomegranate seed-like teeth.

I said, "Come." He looked at me and nodded his head, still holding the door. I advanced a step and said, "Come!" He again nodded his little head. This time I said, "Okay, if you won't come, you would miss something wonderful." I waited for some time. The child let his hand go off the door and slowly started moving, but the moment I stretched my hand out, he immediately ran away. I waited for some time, but he didn't appear. I came back to my room and started sipping the tea with my back to the door when I could feel someone slowly stepping into the room. I deliberately ignored the sound allowing the child to get into the room. There was a hesitant moment of silence. I could feel that he was already in the room and was slowly moving towards the table. Without turning my head, I went on sipping the tea, looking at him from the corner of my eye and marked that he came close to the table keeping his eyes fixed on me. Reaching near the table, he stopped, knocked on the table, and looked at me. I pretended as though I couldn't hear. This time he knocked again, two to three times, more forcefully. I had no other way but to turn my head. And then, we were face to face to each other. He looked at me in fear. I smiled and immediately he gave a full-faced smile, exposing all his tiny teeth and then pointing at the typewriter on the table.

"Could I play it?" he asked. I couldn't follow exactly what he meant by 'play.' So, I just looked at him. He repeated it, "Could I play it?"

I thought it best to allow the child to do what he liked to and said, "Yes, you can."

He seemed to have felt extremely delighted at my consent, but I was surprised that he didn't do what he wanted to, rather kept on looking at me apprehensively.

I said, "What happened? Play!"

He tilted his head to the right and asked, "Could I?"

I said, assuring him, "Yes, play!"

Swaying his curly-haired head repeatedly, he stood up on the chair and stooping over the typewriter started pressing the keys, first with much caution, with a light touch of his little fingers. He did it repeatedly, each time with more and more force and then violently. His eyes were sharply focused on it, but ultimately he seemed to have felt disgusted. In complete disappointment, he looked at me.

I asked, "What happened?"

He said sadly, "It's not playing!" It was only then that I could follow him. He took my typewriter to be some kind of a musical instrument.

I laughed and said, "Oh, you want tung-tyang pmi-pmu?"

The child, with a broad chin and wide eyes, nodded his head, "*Han! Han*!"

I asked, "You like it very much?"

The child nodded again.

I said, "All right, I'll get it for you tomorrow."

At this, he jumped down from the chair and coming close to me said softly, "Would you, really?"

Nobody in my life had ever asked anything from me in such an innocently intimate tone and so I said, "Yes."

But he had doubts still and so asked me, "Sure?"

I promised him, "Yes! Yes! Yes!" But still it seemed he didn't take to my words. So I asked him, "You don't believe me?"

He was candid enough to express his distrust by nodding his head thoroughly and asked me, "You won't be like papa?"

I said, "Why? What did your papa do?"

He came close to me and rubbing his little body against my knees said, "You know, that day I cried for the bus, you know that bus? You don't know? Buddu has one, his papa brought it for him, and that bus you know when you make ghnoo-ghnoo-ghnoo the bus starts rolling and you know there is light in the bus and the light also glows." He stopped for breath.

I said, "Now I understand, you grabbed Buddu's bus, and Buddu won't give it to you, so you started crying, and so your papa said I would get a bus for you. Isn't it?"

The child looked at me in amazement nodding his head with *'haan haan'* and then asked me, "How could you know? You were also there?"

I smiled and said, "Yes! I was also there watching your mischief!"

The child was excited, "You were there!"

I said, "Of course."

And then, punching on my thigh with his small fist, he said, "Then, why didn't you get one for me?" I pretended to have been hit hard. The child looked at my grimaced face guiltily and then snuggled into my arms and said, "I won't hit you any more. Will you get that tung-tyang for me?"

That is how a strange relationship developed between us - that little child and I. Within weeks, I was startled to discover that I was not staying back in the office or in the officers' club till late in the evening. After the office hour, I would come straight to my rented house, and what was more interesting was that on the way to my house I would do a little bit of shopping for vegetables, cooking materials, groceries, and of course, a small can of milk which I would collect from a cow-owner near our house. The most conspicuous thing among all these was the can full of milk. It was finally this "milk-matter" that slowly led the parents of the child to slacken their hold on him. Initially, his parents didn't seem to be happy if the child would come to me or stay with me for a long time. The day I bought the Casio for the child, the parents didn't even try to hide their displeasure at my display of affection for their offspring. It might be that they had read a dubious motive behind my gift for the child. The gift, on my part being a stranger to them and without any specific occasion, was certainly too costly and aroused suspicion. They couldn't take it happily. In fact, the child's father was blunt enough to say that they were accepting it only looking at their child's joy, at his cheerful face, and at the same time, warned me against such ostentatious displays of affection. I had no other way but to keep my mouth shut. First of all because, I had never developed that habit of witty retort. It was my nature that I could never react immediately, and they would attribute it to my contemplative bent of mind. So, I preferred to stay silent at the blunt reaction of the child's father. Rather, I reasoned out that it was not irrational on his part to say what he was saying. After all, what sensible person in the world would offer such an unusually costly gift to a child whose family he is a complete stranger to? And, that, too, without any occasion? And, moreover, even the child was also a stranger to me just two days before?

I realised my idiocy, and so I had to keep mum. The next evening coming from the office, I was making tea when the child came straight to the kitchen, smiled at me, moved around all the rooms, and then asked me, "You have no kids?"

I said, "Kids? Oh, no, I don't have any."

He asked, "Why?"

I said, "Because you're there!"

But, the child asked me, "Then, how shall I play? With whom?"

I said, "Play? Why, I will play with you!"

The child rolled his big eyes from one corner to other and said in astonishment, "You'll play with me?" and he started laughing.

I asked, "Why? Why can't I play with you?"

The child nodded his head seriously and said gravely, "No. You can't. You are big, and I am so small."

I said, "So what? Don't big fellows play with little fellows?"

In utter surprise, he asked, "Do they?"

I said, "Of course."

He then immediately asked, "Why is it then that my papa don't play with me?"

I said, "Your papa would certainly like to play with you, but he mustn't be getting time. He's so busy you know."

At this, he asked, "Then, how is it that you get time to play with me? You aren't busy?"

I assured him, "No, I have time. I 'm not busy."

The child asked, "Why? Why is it that papa is busy and you aren't?"

I had to think for a minute and then said, "No, I am also busy, but not as busy as your papa."

"Why?" he asked.

I said, "Because, your papa has different work, and I have also different work."

He went on asking "Why?" and I went on explaining him, "Because, your papa has a shop. He goes to his shop. I work in an office, and I go to my office, and then office time and shop time are different, so your papa doesn't get time to play with you." But, it seemed the child was not satisfied with any of my explanations.

He came up with the next question, "Why don't papa work in your office?"

I said, "Perhaps he had no idea about my office?"

The child then had the next query, "Why didn't you tell him?"

I said, "How could have I? I didn't know him?"

"Why?"

"Because, I was not here."

"Why were you not here?"

"Because, I was not working in the office."

"Why?"

"Because, I was then reading."

This time, the child asked in astonishment, "You were reading! ABC! You know I have a book and many, many pictures are there! You know apple? I know. A for apple."

I asked, "You like the book?"

The child looked highly pleased and swayed his head.

I asked, "You go to school?"

He shook his head, "But, I will."

"Who teaches you then? Your mama?" I asked.

He said, "*Hnaa*, but Mama doesn't teach me. She says 'read' 'read' and she listens to radio." He then asked me, "Will you teach me?"

I said, "Yes, certainly, you come with your book, and I'll teach you."

"You won't listen to your radio?"

I said, "No. I won't."

He asked, "Why?"

I said, "Because, I don't have one."

"Why?" he asked.

I said, "Because, I haven't bought it."

He asked, "Why? Why haven't you bought it?"

The child's queries were endless. My answers were also equally meaningless. I knew. So, that was how we, the child and I, came close to each other through such meaningless sessions. In fact, it was then that I started wondering about the meaning of "meaning." I remembered how my teacher in the college once had told me, "Things do not exist in this world. You have to make it exist, and that is creativity." What to me appeared meaningless carried so much meaning for the child, and finally, I started noticing that in the process of engaging myself with the meaningless activities of the child, slowly, I was transformed from a depressed, apathetic, morbid person to a lively, cheerful, domestic being. Everybody in the office was surprised to see me so unusually agile and prompt. My boss was highly impressed with my performance.

One day he even joked, "Hello, young man, you look so jolly nowadays!" With a seemingly mischievous smile, he would say, "But, young man! I am not going to grant you leave for marriage!"

To which, I, too, said mischievously, "You need not worry, sir! That, I will manage without leave."

It was then that I started realising how I was changing, and it was again the awareness of change in me that drew me more towards that child. I would not waste even a single moment after the office was closed. I would rush back to my rented house to play with the child. Coming back, first, I would enter the kitchen to make tea and that very moment, turning back, I would see that the child was standing there silently just behind me, and as I would turn back, he would giggle and run away to hide himself, and then it was my turn to find him out with a tumbler full of milk in my hand. My effort would be to look for him here and there, every nook and corner of each room deliberately leaving the spot he would be hiding behind, and then with a great sigh of deep frustration, I would have to slump down on the sofa saying, "Alright, the milk is so tasty today, and my child is so unlucky! Let me have it then." Immediately, before my words were uttered completely, he would suddenly come out from his hiding place rushing towards me.

"No, no, it's my milk…my milk…I would have it!"

It was this habit of having milk regularly that brought his parents closer to me. Once they were to visit one of their cousins, and so his father came to my room looking for his son, and he was startled to see that him sitting comfortably on the sofa, engrossed in luxurious relish of a full tumbler of milk. In utter amazement, he asked me how I could make it happen! First, I failed to get at what he was asking about, and so he explained to me that they had tried their best to make their child drink milk but had failed completely. How could I make it happen?

The reply came pat to me. "Very simple. I never tried. It's just a game that I started playing with him, and he has been enjoying the game. Just, that's it."

This event changed their whole attitude towards me. That day hence I had never seen his parents worrying about their child, if he used to stay with me in the night. Sometimes, he would insist on eating with me at night. He wouldn't listen to his mother's alluring words, and even I would say, "I don't know how to cook. What could he eat?"

He would ask me, "Then, what are you going to eat?"

I would say, "I can manage with something that I can prepare."

The child would then say, "I will also eat what you cook for yourself." He used to be relentless. So, I would have no other way but to take care of cooking something that he could eat which was certainly in the beginning quite a frustrating experience, since I had never in my life entered into the kitchen. So, initially I used to be extremely careful, and what was more inspiring for me, the child would be sitting there in the kitchen silently, intently watching every moment of my activity in the kitchen and even sometimes trying to help me in all the possible ways that he could.

"Match-box? I am getting it."

"You don't know what to do next? Well, let me go ask my mama." Without waiting for me to say anything, he would rush and then running back would say, "Mama asked what's the item you are cooking?"

I would say, "It's not necessary. I can do it."

He would then settle down on the floor crossing his legs and ask me, "You know it?"

I would say, "Yes, you just sit and see how I am making it!"

The child would then suddenly ask, "Why do you know cooking? You don't have your mama?"

I would say, "Yes, it's from my mama that I have learnt it."

He would ask, "Why?"

I would say, "So that I can cook something tasty for this naughty child." At this, he would give a very sweet and pleasant smile. In the process, I had the practice of cooking for myself, and after some months, I felt immensely glad that I was steadily growing independent and had started feeling satisfied and contented. Apathy and indifference had faded out.

I could feel that I was developing a tremendous passion for life.

It was during that time that one day when I entered my office, my boss congratulated me and handed over a sealed letter to me. I looked at him, and he told me that I had been transferred to some other branch on promotion. All my colleagues expressed their genuine happiness since, as they used to say over those few months, I had been changed completely from an irritating, temperamental, and lethargic person to an extremely jolly and loving young man! Everybody in my office was happy at my promotion.

But, I couldn't understand why I myself did not feel that happiness. It was only the day I left that place that I realised why it was so.

Since it was my first job and also the first transfer, I had no idea of how to get the things packed. Perhaps the child's parents, who had been quite chummy with me in those days, could notice this and so offered their help. Two days before my departure, his father came to my house and expressed his surprise, "*Arre*! You haven't yet started packing up!"

I said, "No, I'll do it tomorrow."

"Tomorrow? Do you have any idea how troublesome it is? Do you know how much time it will take? Have you already collected those cartons, fibre strings, gunny bags? Do you have any idea about the materials you would need for packing?" And then taking a look at the things I had then in my rented house, he heaved a sigh and said: "*Arre baap*! You aren't a poor householder, it seems! You are quite a sedate family man! Who would believe you to be a bachelor?"

I blushed and smiled. Even I myself was astonished at my acquisitive domestic instinct, and I knew that it was all because of that child. In the beginning, it was a mere curiosity, and then it was all fun. Later it became an unchallengeable habit, and then it grew into an unknown relationship, and then it came to be our life - mine and the child's.

The day before I was to leave the place, the child's father asked me to take meals at their house since my belongings were packed up, and that, too, with their help. So, when in late evening I went to his house for dinner, the joy in the child's face was a scene to behold. He started jumping, running, rushing to his mother in the kitchen and rushing back to me and informing me the items already prepared and the items to be still prepared and consoling me that it won't take much time, sometimes even asking me, "Are you hungry?"

I would quip, "Yes, very hungry."

He would then rush to the kitchen shouting, "Mama! Mama! Why haven't you cooked the things early? Uncle feels hungry!" And the next moment, we were all surprised and started laughing when he came out of the storeroom with a pot full of puffed rice, offering me like an old granny, "You better take it now. Mama will finish cooking very soon."

The child hardly had an inkling of the truth of life - of comings and goings, of meeting and parting. The next morning when the child woke up, half of my belongings had already been loaded on the mini truck. In fact, I had not thought of hiring a vehicle for my luggage. The child's father laughed at my inexperience and ignorance, "How do you imagine to carry all these things? On the bus-top?" He himself then arranged a mini truck with labourers for loading and unloading. It came very early in the morning, even I was sleeping. I woke up at the sound of the horn. The driver started blowing the horn fiercely. So, I opened the door and saw the child's father standing in front of me with a cup of tea. I felt ashamed and before I could say "sorry" he handed over the cup to me and said, "It's alright. Relax. Relax. You needn't worry. You just tell them what are the things to be loaded, and they will do it."

So, I was sitting on the verandah along with the child's father watching the whole process of loading and sometimes giving instructions to take care in handling the delicate things when the child appeared there waking up from his sleep wearing a lousy look. He came straight to me and snuggled into my lap. It was then that his eyes fell on the truck and also on the labourers carrying luggage from my house. He couldn't understand what was happening. He looked at me blankly and then went into my house, moved around all the rooms, and then went towards the truck, and then, coming over to me, asked, "Why are you giving your things to them?"

I said, "No, I am not giving. They are loading it there."

"What is it they're doing?"

I said, "Putting my things there."

"Why?"

"Because, I will have to move to another place."

"Where?"

"Far away."

"Far away? How far?"

"Far, far away."

"How will you come then?"

"Come? Why?"

At this the child giggled, and twisting his fingers

asked, "How are you going to play then?" He said this in a tone as if he posed a puzzle for me.

I said, "I will find another baby to play with me."

The child suddenly sprang up from my lap, looked at me sternly and then ran away crying loudly at the pitch of his voice. The cry was so piercing that his mother came out to see what had happened. His father told how it was going on humorously.

The mother, too, laughed and lifting him to her arms consoled, "Your uncle is not a good fellow. Very bad. Very bad. He is hurting my cute child! What does he think of himself! Let him go. We don't need such a bad friend for our baby. We will find out another good uncle."

But, before his mother had finished, the child suddenly slipped down from her arms with a heavy jerk and rushing forward to me literally threw himself down on me. Grabbing me in his little hands, he started murmuring: "No. No. You are my uncle. I won't allow any other uncle. Only you will play with me."

I said, "Alright, I will play with you, nobody else."

Immediately, he raised his head and asked me again in that mocking tone, twisting his fingers, "But how? Unless you come over here daily?"

I pretended to give a serious thought to this problem and then said, "Alright then, you better come with me. That will solve the problem."

The boy, to my surprise, pondered seriously over my proposal. Then, he smattered, "But papa, mama, they won't go?"

I said, "*Hnaa*, they will also come, but later, alright?"

He seemed to give another thought to it and then without saying anything to me went to his father and asked him, "Papa, you will also come to his place?"

His papa laughed and said, "*Hnaa! Hnaa*! Sure. Sure."

At this, I noticed, his face lit up brightly and telling me that he would be coming with me, he ran to his mother shouting in joy, "Mama! Mama! I will go with my uncle! I will go with my uncle!"

Is there anything called "fun" for a child? Sometimes I sit and think of it. The loading was almost over when the child came out of my drawing room with a folding umbrella in his hand. I had kept it on a shelf in the drawing room along with my handbag. If it rained, it would be of much help. The child put it cautiously under his armpit. We laughed at his behaviour. When the loading was over, it was almost 10 o'clock. His father told me to have the lunch there with him. When we sat for the lunch, the child, too, sat with us, keeping the umbrella by his side and asked his mother to serve him, too.

His mother said, "No, my baby! You haven't yet taken your bath. You had your milk just now. You take with me." The child started shaking his head, refusing to listen to anything.

His father told his mother, "You don't understand. How can he take meals with you? He is going with his uncle."

His mother pretending seriousness told his child: "Oh! You are going with your uncle? You won't stay with us? Then, I am not going to give you food."

The child immediately denied, "No. No. You and papa will also come later...in the evening...no, Papa?" He turned towards his father expecting him to explain to his mother in details.

His father nodded, "Yes, yes, we will go afterwards."

The real scene started when taking farewell from everybody around there. I got into the truck, and sitting comfortably on the seat stuck my head out for a last hug with the child who was in the arms of his father. Then, I stretched out my hand for the umbrella. The child held it under his arm more tightly and was almost ready to jump from his father's arms into mine.

His father was trying to hold him back when he started shouting, "I'll go with uncle."

His father tried to console him, "*Arre* fool! How can you go in the truck? The uncle will go now and keeping the luggage there, he will come in a very big car, and we all will go in that car."

But, the child was relentlessly shouting, "I'll go with the uncle! I'll go with my uncle!" He wouldn't listen to anybody, to anything. Then, someone suggested to let him go till the end of the street. So, his father pushed him into the truck. Still holding the umbrella under his arm, the child sat on my lap, and with a face filled with limitless joy, he bade farewell to everybody standing there, even to his mother. It was getting late, so the driver didn't want to waste anymore time.

When the truck started to move, the child waved his hand and said, "Mama, don't worry, you will come afterwards. No, Papa?" to which everybody standing there burst into a loud laughter. The child could not understand, but he joined with them. His father took a bicycle and came along with the truck. Reaching the end of the street, the driver stopped the vehicle. His father asked someone there to hold the cycle and stretched his hand to take back the child. The child could not understand anything, and when he realised what was it about, he clung to me, grabbing my neck tightly with his arms and shouting, "I'll go with my uncle! I'll go with my uncle!"

The scene that day I shall never forget in my life. His father alone could not take him back. So, he took the help of two of his acquaintances present there. Three of the stout grown ups then, literally, started snatching and ultimately succeeded in pulling the child from inside the truck, breaking the clutch of his little hands around my neck. With tears overflowing his eyes, he was crying piercingly with all his strength, as if all his anger and despair would split open his throat.

I could hear him crying for a long time, till our vehicle took to the main road.

Four

For a long time after my transfer, I could not sit at my writing table. The heart-splitting, desperate crying of the child haunted me for months. The moment I would sit at my table with a pen in my hand, something in me, an unknown pain, a strange but acute feeling of loss, would not allow me to think of anything else. I sat for hours at my table, blankly, looking in vain at the blank white sheet. It was during this time that my friend came to my place one evening and started asking about the progress of my book. I gave a shrug and said, "Nothing." And then, I added, "But, I have written something about me, and in fact, what I have written about is why I am not able to make any progress on the book." My friend naturally failed to understand what I said so clumsily, and I was clumsy because I myself was not clear about why I was failing to make any progress. So, as expected, my friend wanted to see what I had written.

The next evening he came again and said, "You see, after all, I am a student of literature, and so, as you know, my critical sense is certainly of some practical value. And, my valuable opinion is that your progress is highly satisfactory. Not only satisfactory, it has rather an unusual freshness about it."

I said, "But, it's not there!"

"What do you mean it's not there?" my friend asked.

I said, "I mean it's not a part of that book I am writing. It's about what happened to me. Understand? Me. Me - and not to the character in that book."

My friend looked at me for some seconds and then

said, "All right, all right, I do understand now. It's something about you. You. The author of the book. But then, you know that I am a student of literature, and I would rather suggest that you retain this episode as a part of the book."

My friend stopped and looked at me expecting my view on the suggestion. I was totally confused and so asked, "You mean to say that this episode should form a part of the 'My Autobiography' portion of the book?"

"Exactly."

I said, "But, how could it be? After all, it is my life story! It happened to me! Not to the character in the book? And moreover, I just wrote it down casually, not with an intention of writing. It just came to me. I was feeling very sad, very, very sad after leaving that place. It was troubling me terribly, the way the child clutched to me desperately, and the way he was dragged out. It…it simply kept haunting me, and so whenever I sat down with a pen in my hand, it used to come to the tip of my pen. That's it. That's how it was written, if at all you accept it as some form of writing."

There was a long pause. My friend then broke the silence, "You retain it as an integral part of the book, as a part of 'My Autobiography' of the book. After all, you are the author, the maker. The readers will know that it happened to the character in the book, not to you. And, stylistically, too, you see, you have written in the first person. No problem. You just transport it from your life to the life of your character, and the matter is over."

And this is how the preceding chapter about the child was made to form a part of "My Autobiography."

The confusion stayed for a pretty long time. I couldn't make any progress. One day, I told my friend about my confusion. He didn't take it seriously. Brushing aside all my problems like flitting away the flies on the table, he said gravely, "Don't worry. Carry on."

I said, "You see, my specific problem is that I feel I am getting confused about my own personal life and the life of my characters in the book I am writing. You see, I have started feeling that it's either me getting into the lives of my invented characters, or perhaps it's like my characters have started encroaching into my own life. You see?"

My friend stopped me short and said calmly, "Doesn't matter. It may work either way."

I protested, "What do you mean 'either way?' You don't know how I am gradually losing my sense of existence! The reality of my existence! Sometimes I feel awful about the whole thing. I have started doubting myself. Is it that I am slowly getting metamorphosed into a fictional character?"

My friend laughed at my fear and said, "That's the way an ordinary man grows into a great writer. John Keats calls it 'the negative capability,' the quality that makes a writer great. Shakespeare had it, and that's why Shakespeare is great." He added, with a naughty smile: "Who knows? One day you will also be a great writer like Shakespeare, and in fact, you have started showing the signs of it!"

I just listened to what my friend said, didn't make any further comment, nor tried to make him understand me. I knew that he was not able to appreciate my situation, my agony, that the products of my own imagination possessed me, that they had started overpowering me. And that I am steadily losing my capability of keeping away the sufferings of my characters exclusively as their sufferings.

It was during this state of my anguish that I wrote the next chapter of the Book.

Five

I was passing through the most sedative days of my life when one day I got a letter from a friend and a money-order, too. Those were the days when two shocking deaths in my life had turned me so stunningly inward that everybody started worrying that I was going neurotic. Possibly, I was. In spite of myself, I was not able to erase from memory, my father's awful end, nor the slow suicide, a gruesome revenge, of my loved one. I felt blankness all around me. A sense of abandoned desolation. When the deliverer handed over the letter to me, I just took it from him and, without caring to look at it, went to my room and threw it on the table. It fell on the floor. I didn't try to pick it up. Letting it lie there, I straightaway fell flat on the cot. Soon, I got bored staring at the drab ceiling. I turned on my side when my dull eyes fell on that letter, and the colour and the size of the cover drew my attention. It was an aerogramme from abroad. I felt curious. Who could write to me from abroad? I got up from the bed and picked up the letter and found that it was from my friend who was working in the US. I opened the letter, and when I finished reading it, I not only found it interesting but very intriguing as well. My friend had requested me to hand over a lump sum amount of money to his mother in the village. But, what was interesting about it was that I had to convince his mother to accept it. The reason was that over these months, the money he had been sending to his mother used to go back to him, refused by her. My friend had expressed his anguish and was also worried about her living alone in the village without any other source of livelihood. She had also no one else to fall back on or to go to in a time of need. So, my friend in the US had entrusted me with that "noble" task of "saving" the life of an "unfortunate" mother.

I should admit that the task, whether noble or not, attracted me instantly. First of all, I thought that it would somehow or other make up for the loss of two lives in my life. And secondly, that in the process of "saving" a life I might get back to my normal way of life.

I didn't waste any more time. The very next day, I set out on a journey to my friend's village. Truly speaking, he was never my friend. At least, I never took him as my friend. He was merely my classmate, though I had been to his village sometimes. But, he used to look upon me as his only friend. Perhaps I was, since he was never so close to anybody else of our class as he was to me. That might have led him to treat me as his friend. His mother, also, I knew, had the same impression. It might be because she had never seen her son with anybody else other than me. And, that was why when he after his study here wanted to go abroad for further study, his mother asked me to convince her son not to. But, it came out to be the other way round. Instead of dissuading her son, rather I tried to persuade her to agree to her son's wish. She fumed. When I started to convince her that it was for a bright future of her son, she flared up.

"Why don't you go and make your future bright?"

To which I told her that I had never been a bright student in my life. I somehow managed to pass in the exams whereas her son had an excellent career, and naturally therefore, he should have big ambitions. She listened to me but didn't say anything.

Later that day, while serving meals, his mother asked, "What is that big ambition? Study is over, now get a job and a *bohu*, have your own family, raise your children, and be happy. *Bbaass*! This is all what I know about life. This is what my parents knew. And their parents. And their parents, too. What is that nonsense you talk about? I don't understand. It doesn't get into my head, big ambition, bright future. All *bakbass*."

My friend was going to argue, but I made him stop. His mother sat for some time in silence and then went away to the kitchen to fetch more rice, when I told my friend that it was better to let his mother speak out her mind freely and that we should rather wait for an opportune time to make her agree, preferably when she would be emptied of all her arguments.

I was surprised when that very evening his mother gave in, in tears though. I was sitting on the inner verandah of the house. My friend's mother came out from inside the low-roof worshipping-room in the courtyard with an earthen lamp on one palm and the other palm over it to ward off the breeze, her wrinkled face glowing in the flame of the lamp. She placed it on the platform of the *tulsi*-plant kneeling down on her knees.

The village evening has its own character. In those days, there was no electricity, nor the television, and it was only in some houses of a few better off people that one could hear the programme on the radio. The entire village, otherwise, would suddenly sink into an eerie silence. The placid lucidity of the twilight hour would all of a sudden be lost in a thick black animal-like darkness. The bizarre silence and darkness then would cast a spell of misty charm, leading, if one likes, to a strange state of contemplation, of a weird and wonderful sensation, of a different pulsation of life.

It was when I was sitting there alone in such a contemplative mood, totally engrossed, that my friend's mother came up to me and sitting on the edge of the verandah asked me straight, "What do you think to be better?"

I was in such a state of mind that I couldn't hear what she said. So, I just gazed at her. She repeated what she had said and looked up anxiously. I didn't know how a kind of abstruse philosophical uttering came out of me, "See *mousi*. Look at this evening. Feel this 'now.' It sets a different mood. Neither this evening nor this moment was there during the midday. It's altogether different. This is what we say 'nature,' natural, anything that goes against it is 'unnatural.' The moment 'now' appeals, because it is natural. Isn't it? Nature takes its own course. Who are we to dictate to it?"

Perhaps I ran out of my thoughts or musings, or perhaps there was no need for any further talk. So, I stopped. I noticed my friend's mother, too, perhaps had no need for any words. She fell into a resigned silence, sat there with me for a long time, and then stood up and went away silently.

And, that was how my friend went abroad for higher study with his mother consenting to sell whatever cultivating land they had for arranging the money he needed. But, what was heartening for his mother was that immediately after his study he took up a job there and got married to an American woman. Since then, he had been sending the money to his mother, and his mother was going on refusing it.

My journey to his village on his request therefore was a kind of mission, a mission to save the life of an unfortunate mother languishing in poverty and isolation, in loss and lonesomeness. I felt inspired.

On my way to his village, I was simply thinking of my so called friend. During those days when he was still pursuing his study there in the US, sometimes he would post some interesting letters narrating his intimacy with an American girl. In one of those letters, he asked me to send a note on Indian Upanishads. His girlfriend, I have forgotten the name he had mentioned, was, as he had stated, keenly interested in Indian philosophy. Even in another letter, he wrote that his girlfriend would like to visit India. She had developed a passion for India, and that, he had written, "I confess and I regret that I am quite ignorant of my own country. She asks me such questions about India and Indian way of thinking that I feel embarrassed. Now I realise that I haven't had any education at all. I have wasted my life only in mugging up some readily available notes and nothing else. Do you know, one day I was literally in tears when my girlfriend wanted to know from me the story of the two golden birds in the Upanishads. What is that story? Do you have any idea about it? Could you send that story to me?"

Funny. That was exactly what I thought, funny. How could I know the story of the two golden birds? Did I ever read Sanskrit or philosophy as my subjects in graduation? I know that he knew it very well. Even then, he had asked me to send him the story. Sheer stupidity! I thought and remained silent. Just a week after I got another letter written in a language with intense impatience and passion asking me to let him know whether our ancestors were "Ariyans" and were "outsiders?" Not "insiders?" Not from inside India?

Awfully interesting! But, when the next week I got two letters, one after another, frenetically imploring me to send him notes on those funny queries, it made me feel disgusting. Has he gone mad! I thought so and kept silent. Curiously, there were no more letters from him, nor any news. I felt relieved and was glad that finally he had got over that silly passion. Just a week after, I got a single-line letter, "My girlfriend has broken away from me. Got married to another boy."

When I reached the village of my friend, it was almost past midday. I was feeling hungry. I had taken something as breakfast very early in the morning when I came out from my house. Getting down from the train, I stood there on the platform roving my eyes for a food stall or something of the sort. It was a small station, a very small village station, and so usually a very few passengers would board or get down. Even those who get down, they head straight for their village home. There is, of course, one gate there for both exit and entrance, and one would hardly see passengers using that gate, since there are as many trodden paths as there are villages nearby in different directions. Last time, when I had come with my friend, we had taken one of those paths reaching his village straight. Standing there, on the middle of an almost empty platform, I could neither spot a stall nor could decide which path to take to reach his village. But, somehow or other, I could remember that there was a kind of tea stall outside the platform where we had taken *pakodas* along with tea. My friend had come to see me off, and the train was late, and so we were trying to pass time. I could also recollect that the stall was just near that only gate of the platform. So, without wasting anymore time, I walked straight for the gate, and coming outside, I felt extremely delighted to locate the stall. But, when I reached the stall, the scene was disappointing. The stall was wearing an empty look. No customers. Only on one side, under its shadow, a group of aged people, engrossed in playing cards, silently, with occasional shouts of joy. I couldn't decide what to do. There was no one inside the stall. Since it was already past midday, naturally no customer would come for *tiffin* or tea. I stood still in front of that stall and then a bare-bodied man with a shabby loin-cloth around his waist who was pleasantly watching the card-play looked at me and asked in a guttural voice, "Yes sir, what happened?"

I looked at the man and then mumbled something like *tiffin*.

The man obviously couldn't hear me, and so he came forward closer to me and asked again, "Yes sir, what happened?"

I fumbled, "No, I thought I would get…get something to eat."

The man laughed and said, "It's not the time. You can't get anything to eat at this hour of the day." And then, throwing a thorough look at me, he asked, "Coming from the town?" I nodded my head. "You don't appear to be of this locality?" I again nodded my head. "Which village you are to go? To whom?" I told him the name of my friend and his village. The man's eyes got screwed up, "Who?" I again told the name of my friend. The man this time gave a suspicious look at me. I felt embarrassed. He asked, "In what way you are his relation?"

I said, "No, I am not his relation."

"Not relation? Then what?"

I said, "He happens to be my friend. We were reading in the same college."

At this, the man seemed to have been satisfied a bit. "*Hnaa!*" He made an appreciative gesture and dusting the bench with his dirty oily towel that was hanging on his shoulder, he asked me to sit there and then taking his usual seat inside the stall asked me again, "Which village you said?" I repeated the name of the village. The man again screwed up his eyes, thought over something, and then with a broad grin said: "*Hnaa*! Now I understand the boy you have come to." But, the next moment he became grave and affecting seriousness in tone asked, "Are you his real friend?"

I had no idea what exactly was on his mind about the word friend, but, since from my own side I had never taken him to be my friend, I hesitantly replied, "No, not friend exactly... but..."

The man stopped me short, "*Hnaa*! That was exactly what I have guessed. My guess can never be wrong. You know? For how many years I have been here with my stall?" He put the question and looked at me with his mouth wide open. It was so wide that I could clearly see all his bacteria-infected black, uneven, un-enameled teeth along with the swollen ungainly upper part of them. And then came answer from inside that mouth, "You were not even born then." Saying this, he changed his sitting posture to a more comfortable position. I could apprehend that he was now going to narrate a long story, almost his autobiography.

I was feeling so hungry that I could not check myself, and before he could gather himself to start his life story I said blatantly, "The matter is I feel terribly hungry, and I was looking for something to eat somewhere."

Perhaps there was some kind of helplessness in my tone that appealed to the man. He seemed to be really taking pity on me. Without saying anything, he got up, surveyed the inside of some utensils, lifting their lids, and smiled at me, "Well, there is something left, but I don't know whether you'd like it. After all, you are from the town, used to nice meals!"

His mere words delighted me so much that I immediately smiled back and addressing him as my mother's sister's husband said, "*Mausa*! Anything will do. My entire stomach is burning now, it can consume anything."

The man nodded his head, "I understand. I understand

your plight well. I can serve you only with plain rice and dough of mashed potato. That is what I have now left over from the meals I prepared for four to five regular customers." Saying this with all tenderness in his tone, he placed a piece of banana leaf there on one side of the bench I was sitting on and then poured the rice on it, and just as I was going to gulp a palm full of rice, he happily said that he had some green chilly and raw onion, too, and that it would add to the taste of the plain rice.

It did. In fact, it did in a very strange way. I was relishing the simple food, and his story, too.

"You know? Your friend you have come to was not even born when I started this stall. That was the time when this railway station was inaugurated. The minister came, and there was a huge gathering here, and my father brought me along with his utensils for making tea and *tiffin* here. He had a very nice business that day. He later told me, that day his sale was such that he had never been able to earn so much in his whole lifetime. And so, he made me sit here to help him. People told that the railway station would give us a roaring business. And so, I am here from that day. The details of all the people in the locality are at the tip of my fingers. Now you understand? When you said you have come to your friend, I doubted you. After all, do you know that your friend isn't here? He is there in some foreign country? Only his mother stays, alone."

I nodded my head in affirmation and said, "In fact, I have come to his mother."

The man in the shop asked, "To his mother? Why?"

I felt hesitant. Should I say that I have come to hand over the money sent by his son? Would it be proper to say? What impression would he have on my friend? And, his relationship with his mother? So, I said, "Just to see her. I used to come with my friend when we were reading in the college. I thought I hadn't come for a long time to see her. She must be feeling lonely. So, I thought let me go and see how she is! She would feel happy too."

I stopped and looked up to see whether he believed in what I said and found that the man in the shop was looking at me with his mouth wide open, his face expressing an utter sense of astonishment. His gaze stayed on me for some minutes, and then with a broad smile spreading across his whole face he said, "God bless you, my son! God bless you! You have rightly said she would be happy! What to speak of happiness? She would feel terribly delighted! She would start dancing! That bastard son of hers! Do you know what her condition is now? Terrible! Terrible! I cannot describe it. You can't stand it if I start narrating her misery. Very well! Very well that you have come! God has sent you. You are her God-sent son!"

The man stopped to take a long breath and then with a swaying of his head expressed his own happiness, "I am very happy! I myself feel very happy to learn that at least God is there to take care of the wretched on this earth!" Saying this, he folded his hands and looked up at the sky above.

I started feeling embarrassed and ashamed, too. I knew under what compulsion I had come and for what purpose! And so, in order to avoid further embarrassment, making payment for the meal, I collected my bag and stood up, thanked the man a lot, and even stooped a bit in the posture of paying respect to the age and also to the sense of affection and homeliness that he had generated in such a natural way.

I was about to leave the place when he called me back: "*Hnaa*! Listen, my son! If you can, try to help that old lady. She is craving for a *darshan* of her *Kalia*! She is mad to have a glimpse of Lord Jagannath on the Chariot on the day of *Gundicha*. If you can, it is my request to you. Take that old lady to *Purusottam*. She will be so happy that your whole life would be blessed with joy!"

I listened to what he said and without saying anything or making any gesture of response started walking straight towards the village of my friend.

It was late afternoon. The sun had gone down, but was yet to set. The tall coconut trees on both sides of the uneven trodden path of the village cast long shadows and were also making the setting sun play hide and seek with me. A strange mellowness hung in the air. When I reached the house of my friend, it was the hour of *godhuli*, the hour of cows returning from the field raising dust all along the village and the raised dust-particles against the mild pink-coloured sunshine were weaving visuals of mysticisms all around.

I knocked at the door. There was no response. I banged the door. Still no response. Some village boys, playing at a distance, caught sight of me and shouted from there, "Not home! She isn't home. Might be in the temple."

I looked back at them and asked: "Where is the temple?" One of the boys came running to me and showed the way to the temple.

The evening was yet to settle in. The temple was empty. A small temple, it was on something like a mound with a few stairs to climb up, surrounded by a decaying boundary. I entered the boundary hesitantly. It hadn't anything like a gate or an entrance. Nothing of the sort. There were some parts of the compound wall which had collapsed or where stones had come off making cleavages. The place wore a deserted look, except some trees here and there inside the boundary. As I hesitantly entered through one of those openings, my eyes fell on a scantily clad bare-bodied old man lying on his back under the long afternoon shadow of a tree. Perhaps he was the regular priest of the temple. I went to him straight and asked if he had seen the old mother of my friend. I told the name of my friend.

The man got up and said, "Oh! That old lady! Poor fellow! Where else could she go? She must be somewhere here, somewhere around this temple." As he was saying, he rose to his feet and asked me, "But, my son! Who are you? I haven't seen you before? Which village you are from?"

I said, "No, I am not from any village. I happen to be a college friend of her son."

At this, the old priest, sweeping his fingers across his sacred thread slinging from the shoulder, asked gruffly, "That bastard son! That motherfucker! The scoundrel is wallowing in luxury there abroad, fucking the white-skinned women there, and look at the wretchedness of his mother here! But why have you come, after all? What work you have with her?" The man gave me an indignant look.

I had no particular answer to such questions. Again, I started feeling embarrassed. The priest gave me a scrupulous look and waving his hand towards the back of the temple said, "See there. Might be asleep under the tree."

I gave a thankful look at him and without any words went forward towards the back of the temple. From a distance, I could see the old lady, the mother of my friend, a scrawny body only, almost skeletal, looking at the twittering bird on the tree in front. I went close to her. The sun was yet to set, and so my long shadow fell from the side. Following the shadow, she looked up and saw me. I bent down to touch her feet, and as I rose up to my feet, she said, strangely, without any sense of surprise, "When did you come?"

The calm in her tone stunned me, as if she was just waiting for me. And, the next moment, I was completely wonderstruck when she, with a smile in her wrinkled face, said, "I knew you were coming. But, why did you reach so late?"

In fact, I felt totally blank. Her behaviour rendered me absolutely speechless. I stayed standing, silently, like a statue, thinking how could she know that I was to come? Is she in her sanity? Has she gone mad? Even as I was thinking of going back to the priest to ask him if she had gone mad, she rose up from the flat stone she was sitting on and said, "Let's go. You must be feeling hungry. You are so late. Of course, I have everything in my house. I had collected them from yesterday." She was talking and walking very fast. I found it hard to follow her. I almost had to run. And, as we came to the front of the temple, the priest was still there. She pointed her finger at him and said, "I had also collected *ghee* from the priest. He asked me why do you need *ghee*? You are getting *prasad* here?" Saying this, she spread a queer smile in her face and said, "The poor fellow doesn't know that not for me. I wanted it for my son!"

Son! It struck me again. Gone insane? I was thinking what to do when the priest shouted at us, "Going home, *mousi*? Do come in the evening for *prasad*."

At that, the old lady shouted back in an unnaturally cheerful way, "No! No! I'm not coming today. I will have to cook for my son."

The priest shouted back, "Don't worry. I'll give *prasad* for him, too."

I was surprised at the way the old lady reacted to those words of the priest, "Hey! You Brahmin lad! What do you think of my son! *Ynaa*? Living on alms? *Ynaa*? Don't dare open your mouth again! Understand? *Hnaa*!"

She turned back and started walking faster, leaving the priest wondering with his mouth wide open.

While having meals that night, I could be sure that she hadn't gone mad, that she was completely in her senses, that she could clearly recognise me as the friend of her son, and that's what surprised me most. How could she know that I was to come? Had she got any letter from her son? About the money he had sent to me? I was thinking if she knew all about that then I would not have any problem in handing over the money. My difficulty would be over. But, the next moment it struck me if that was the case, then why did my friend send such a letter to me at all?

As all such confusing thoughts started crowding into my mind, the old woman said on her own, "Do you know why I was expecting you?"

Heaving a deep sigh, I looked up at her. It was exactly the question that was troubling me so much. She said, "You see, I would like to go to my *Kalia*, Lord Jagannath. If only once, I could reach Him, He would take me into His embrace, and I would get my salvation! I would be very happy that my life was worth living!"

First, I failed to understand what exactly she meant by what she was saying. I looked at her intently. She seemed to be lost in a dream.

She went on musing, "I approached some of the old men of our village whether they are going to the *Gundicha*, and if they are, whether I could accompany them. But, all of them avoided me. Didn't say anything clearly. I know they aren't willing to take up the responsibility of an old woman."

She stopped, and then suddenly, her face lit up when she said, "But, I remembered you, and God knows how it came to me that you are coming, and see! You came!" She looked up at the sky with folded hands and nodded her head gladly.

I was speechless. I have never seen a face with such bliss and innocence.

The next day, I reached Puri, the land of Lord Jagannath. There was a heavy rush in the train because of the *Gundicha*, the famous Car Festival of Lord Jagannath, two days after. When the train pulled in, I found it beyond me to make the old woman board the train. All my pushing, jostling, elbowing, and shouting failed miserably. The compartments were so packed up to the entrance door that one could hardly make out a space for putting even one foot on the doorstep. But strangely, just at that moment, I saw the man of the tea stall behind me, and before I could speak, he lifted both of us in his two arms and almost threw us into the compartment.

When we reached Puri, the situation looked no better. It was even worse. The platform was full of teeming pilgrims. Not that all of them got down from the train we came by. Most of them were rather seen resting - some lying on their back, some sleeping, some snoring, and some sitting in a group and chatting. I found it extremely difficult to make way to the exit. I thought the old woman must have been feeling sickened at all these. But, when I looked back, I was surprised that the old woman was brimming with joy. Her wrinkled old face seemed to be glowing. I tried to bring her attention to the difficulties we were going to face for accommodation. Immediately came her sharp reply, "Why? Don't I have a place to stay?"

"Where?" I asked.

"Don't worry. Come with me." And then, she led me in a rickshaw to a dingy lane where, getting down from the rickshaw, she picked up a quarrel with the rickshaw puller about the fare in such a raised voice that not only the people from inside the house we were standing in front of but even people from other houses of the lane started crowding around us. I felt embarrassed at the scene and uncomfortable on the swampy place we were standing on. The next moment, however, I felt relieved when a bald-headed, elderly person emerging from the front house greeted my friend's mother and rescued us from the embarrassment and discomfort.

Entering the house, my friend's mother introduced the elderly person to me as her loving brother and then turning towards him said, "Do you know what my son said? He said, 'There's such a crowd here. Where are you going to put up yourself?' And then I told him don't worry, come with me. I have my loving brother here." She said and then started laughing to the fullness of her heart, like a child, which made the whole family burst into a rapturous laughter.

I do not have any idea about what kind of atmosphere was there in that house, but I noticed that my friend's mother exuded such an air that everybody in the family looked so jolly and cheerful. She was sitting on the cot, and all the members of the family from the six-year-old child to the sixty-year-old father of the elderly person, circled around her and were getting amused with every word that she was uttering.

Addressing her as his elderly sister, the old father of the elderly person asked her, "*Alo apa*! Is it true what I hear about your son that he got married to a *memsahib* there and isn't caring for you anymore?"

To which she flared up, "Why! Don't I have another son here to take care of me! Do I ever bother for who does what! I have my *Kalia*. He would look after me!"

Everybody there went into silence at the emotional outburst of the old woman. And, in that silence, I saw, almost all eyes were on me with a silent question: Who is this young man? How could he be another son of this old woman?

I felt embarrassed sitting under their curious gaze. So, I got up and said, "I am going to the beach." I paused and then said: "I'll be back in a while."

I was making for the door when the old woman called me back, "Hey! You know the way here?"

I said promptly, "Yes, I do."

The old woman said, "Look! Don't go for a bath in the sea."

I nodded my head and came out to the street. I sat at the beach till late evening. The sun was already up in the sky, but because of the thick cloud cover, it was not visible, and that lent the view above the sea an extraordinary charm. With the sunshine reflected back from the black cloud, the whole sky was glowing with a soft whiteness. Below it, the deep calm blue sea at a far distance, and in front of me the frolicking children, romantic couples, frenzied youth, a host of shaven-headed old men and women cuddled together in the toe-deep saline water of the sea, all trying to feel and enjoy the roaring waves and breakers in their own ways.

I stayed sitting alone, aloof, taking a dispassionate look at the world before me, occasionally disturbed by the nagging peddlers selling marine objects. I took them as an essential part of the whole scene, forming, I thought, a foil to the fleeting moments of bliss of those engrossed people and the charm of nature that lay before me.

Sitting apart, I experienced the whole world and its nature, too. It was not a universe, but a multi-verse that I could see before me: a bundle of contraries and contradictions, a complex juxtaposition of the beauty and the beast, a splash of colours of the mundane and sublime, all against an infinite stretch of deep blue water of the vast sea, which, through its noise and calm, fascination and ferocity, with its constant process of change from the mellow purple of the morning, the rising sparkling waves against a chalk-white horizon of the noon, to the exquisite scene under the splash of a vermilion sky in the evening, was mocking at the hollowness of that multiverse.

Nothing remains, not even the sea, its waves emerge and dissolve.

The only sense that you can have, sitting idly at the seashore, that life is nothing but a big nonsense. And, what is most funny about it is that the moment you begin to have this sense of nonsenseness you really start living your life.

Funny!

I could not think of anything else the next evening when along with her loving brother, I had to carry on my shoulder the dead body of the old woman, the widowed mother of my friend, the very life I was supposed to "save."

I don't exactly remember how it all came to happen.

The next day was the day of the Car Festival of Lord Jagannath. When I woke up, it was not even the morning. The sun was yet to rise. But, getting up from my bed, I saw that the old lady was visibly angry with me for being so late. Her lovely brother told me that she had made herself ready even long before the daybreak and was restlessly pacing up and down the house.

I said, "But, what is there to hurry about? The *pahandi* isn't going to start before 10 o'clock, after all?"

To which her brother replied, "You can't understand her mind. She is impatient to see the Lord, her Kalia, as she says."

I nodded. "I know. I know. Or else, why should I have brought her here? But what I feel...I think...I mean, as I have been watching her over these last few days, it seems she is steadily losing her sanity."

Her loving brother fixed his eyes on me for a few minutes and then said with all seriousness, "Yes, that is exactly what I also wondered first, but I can tell you now she isn't. She is in complete sanity. I have no doubt about it now." There was an unusual kind of firmness in his tone, and that surprised me.

But since I was not so intimate with them, nor was I any relation of the old lady, I thought I shouldn't enter into any more arguments about it. So, I remained silent and then got up to take my bath.

When I reached the temple, along with the old mother of my friend, the place was yet to take on the look of a gorgeous spectacle. Three tall marvelously colourful chariots meant for three deities - Lord Jagannath, his elder brother Lord Balaram, and their younger sister Devi

Subhadra - were already in front of the temple. The deities were yet to be brought from the temple in the ritual procession.

The old mother of my friend went and laid herself prostrated on the ground before the chariot meant for Lord Jagannath. When she got up to her feet I said, "*Mousi*! There is no god on the chariot! Whom did you pray to?"

At which she spread an enigmatic smile over her face and said, "Are stupid! You can't understand. God is there, everywhere. It's only that you must have eyes to see Him."

Since I had nothing else to do but to escort her, I started playing jokes with her faith. I asked, "What did you pray for?"

She said, "Nothing."

"Nothing?"

"Yes, nothing."

"What were you doing then lying prostrated on the ground?"

"I wasn't doing anything."

It all appeared like a riddle to me. I asked, "What were you exactly doing then?"

She said, "*Arre* stupid! It wasn't like doing anything. What I did was a visible act of surrendering."

I immediately grasped it, "*Haaan*! There you are! You 'did' surrender yourself."

She took a strong exception to it. "No! Not at all. You cannot 'do' surrender. It cannot be done."

I saw that I was gradually getting drawn into a baffling situation. It was beyond my grasp to get at what exactly she was trying to explain.

The old lady could notice my baffled state. So, she tried to explain, "Listen, my boy. Surrendering means you give up yourself, and once you give up something, it does not exist for you. No? Similarly, the moment you surrender, you stop existing. If you say 'I did surrender myself,' it means 'you.' Who did the surrendering is separate from the 'self surrendered.' It means you are still a 'doer.' But, how can you be both a doer and the surrendered self simultaneously? How is it possible to give up yourself and exist at the same time?"

I just looked at her foolishly. Again, she smiled and said, "See? It's very simple. Suppose you have given up smoking. You cannot smoke and at the same time say that I have given up smoking. Is it possible? Giving up smoking means smoking is no more there in you. Surrendering yourself means you are no more there in you."

"So, you have to die!" I exclaimed to tease her more to enter into a dialogue that I found funny but interesting, nonetheless.

She said, "*Arre! Pagla*! Why should you die? Rather you start living."

I naturally failed to understand. I went on looking at her blankly.

She resumed, "The moment you surrender you lose your own identity. Whatever you do, you do with this or that identity as a son, as a friend, as a neighbour, as a student, as a professional, as a local man, as somebody. All your activities are 'your' doings. You are the doer, and so it is you who shall have to bear its results, pain or pleasure, sufferings or joy, whatever it may be. You cannot hold someone else responsible for your doings, after all. Say fate or God!"

As I was still looking at her foolishly, she said: "There is no doer-ship in surrender. You and to whom you surrender become one. It's only then that you have the real living. A true lover can sacrifice his life for his beloved. Why? Because in love duality disappears. There isn't anymore separate identity for them. They become one. And, that's love. And, when you are in Love, you are in surrender."

I nodded, as though I could ultimately grasp the whole thing and said amusingly: "*Hnaa*! Now I understand. It's a very clever way of escaping life, shirking responsibility, doing nothing, shrewdly leading a passive life like a parasite. Isn't it?"

Stroking on my back, she said, "*Dheett pagla*! How can you be at all passive? Remember that every moment you are 'in act.' You cannot live without acting out. That is what you say 'doing.' The very fact that you are breathing is the sign of life. Breathing is an activity. It gives you the message that you are active. It is you who is doing the act of breathing. It's not that somebody else will breathe for you, could it be?"

I simply looked at her amazed.

She took a breath and then resumed, "I understand what you want to express, But it's not passivity, my son! It may appear like that, but in reality, it's just the contrary. There is rather more activity, vigorous activity, but not with passion, with dispassion, rather. It's called detachment. In The Bhagavad-Gita, Lord Krishna makes Arjuna understand this ultimate and the simple truth of life: act without attachment. It's almost as living like water-drops on the lotus leaves. They are there on the leaves but don't ever stick to the leaves. You are not attached. You are not hooked to anything. Since there is nothing to be hooked to, you are free. You have the freedom to create your life, and since there is no attachment, you don't have a past, too. You have only a present, a perpetual present moment only. You have the freedom to create each moment of your life, and when you create, you are happy. You start living. You are in love with life. Desire is not love. Desire is attachment. Love dissolves in desire. In dispassion only does love grow. And, when you are in love, you are in freedom, and you are in surrender. That is called life."

She fell into silence.

For a long time then, I was in a state of awed silence.

The place had started getting crowded. Wherever you looked, you can see only heads, innumerable heads, moving like waves in the sea. The whole scene had taken the look of a sea, a vast sea of people, varieties of people: haggardly poor, well-dressed rich, sloppy middle class, saffron-clad holy men, stupefied devotees, police personnel in uniform, white-clad volunteers, peddlers, snatchers, pickpockets - all sorts of people - men, women, curious children, and young mischief-makers.

And all around, it was buzzing with noise, varieties of noise: running commentary of the entire rituals, announcements for missing persons, peddlers' pitched shouting for their sales, devotees screaming out their awed sense of joy or singing out devotion, swaying and dancing, the rhythmic sound of cymbals and chanting - all sorts of noise getting drowned into one another.

I was overwhelmed and lost in the fabulous spectacle.

Suddenly, I was jerked into consciousness by piercing shouts and frightened screaming all around. The chariot had just started to be pulled when it was forced to a halt. I looked towards it, towards a melee where policemen and volunteers were seen rushing down. The crowd was shouting, "Gone! Gone! Dead! Dead!"

It was only when I saw the volunteers pulling out an unconscious body from under the chariot-wheels of Lord Jagannath that it struck me that the old lady was not there by my side!

I madly tried to rush to the sight but was mercilessly pushed and jostled back. I caught sight of the volunteers with a stretcher scurrying through the crowds towards the nearby hospital. It was so difficult to move through the crowd that I lost sight of the volunteers.

When I reached the hospital, she had already been declared dead.

The dead body was lying there with the face covered in a white cloth, surrounded by some volunteers. I uncovered the face, and yes, it was she, the old widowed mother of my friend.

I slumped there on the floor, dumb. One of the volunteers came to me, put his hand on my shoulder, patted, and asked, "Your mother?" I just nodded my head without any thought. He took some time and then said softly, "She is fortunate enough. She got her deliverance."

After some moments of silence, another volunteer came to me and asked, "Are you a local?" I shook my head in negative. He asked, "Do you have anybody else here at Puri, anybody known or any relative?"

I said, "Yes."

He said, "Well, you can give the address. We will get him here to help you." I told them the address of her loving brother.

After all the formalities were over, helped by some of

the volunteers, we both carried her dead body on our shoulders to the cremation ground.

The cremation ground at Puri has a significant name: *Swargadwar* or The Gateway to Heaven. It is on the beach.

Against the backdrop of a vast sea and a limitless sky, I consigned her to flames.

I do not know if I "saved" her.

Six

Now, I must confess that I have been in a fix for months since I wrote the last sentence of the previous chapter of my novel. Some months, almost a whole year, I suppose, or it might be more, I am not sure, have elapsed in the meantime. Frankly speaking, I had abandoned writing that novel.

I myself do not know why or how it happened. It's only that I remember how after writing the last sentence of that chapter of my novel I started feeling uneasy. Extremely uneasy. Uncomfortable. It was certainly absurd, ridiculous, to think that what I was writing about was real. Not that I did not know that it was not. It was all a fiction, a product of my own imagination. I was fully aware of it. But then...

It's that stupefying "but then" that started haunting me. All the while, the view of a helpless old widow consigned into flame would flash across my eyes.

After a year or so, somehow or other, I could gather myself to resume the writing of my novel. And as I was carrying on, I found that it was not coming to me that fluently as it used to happen earlier. Even in the beginning, after a paragraph or so, my pen would stop, and it wouldn't move any further. I would then keep sitting there, silently. The imagined face of that widow would show up before my eyes, and a muffled sense of grief would seize me. It would go on like this for days, even sometimes for weeks.

Often, I would laugh at myself, at my feelings, and at

my own funny stupidity of grieving over something that was never real. That did not exist at all!

It was in this process that I wrote what I thought to be the end of the novel.

But then, in the meanwhile, I personally got caught up in certain interesting but bizarre situations in my real life. It might appear ironic, but significantly, the writing of the end of my novel was proceeding along with those phenomenal events in my real life, shaking the whole perception of my life so violently that I was in a state of utter confusion, such a stupefying confusion that I failed to sift the real from the unreal, and the unreal from the real.

So, I decided that I would put in everything here in this book: The Proposed End of my Novel, my involvement in the events of my "real" refugee-friend, my accidental entanglement with the child with whom once I had developed intimacy, and finally, addressing to the problems of my own love when I happened to come across her once years after her marriage.

The Proposed End to My Autobiography

It was an idle summer noon of the end of a turbulent period of the 70's. I was alone in my house. My mother was away in Bangladesh. Mujibur's war with Pakistan had just come to an end with the emergence of an independent Bangladesh. During the war, a number of our relations there had taken shelter in our rented house here. During their stay, I had taken some of them to the plot of my father's half-constructed house. They liked the landscape, went around the plot, cheered at the abandoned openness of the locale, the small hills at a distance, and felt happy about the whole scene. But, the older persons among them asked my mother, "How are you going to stay here?"

Failing to get at the import of the question, my mother asked, "Why?"

They were surprised. "What, 'why'? It's such a lonely place! No close neighbours. No community of your own. All strangers. No river. No coconut trees. No life!"

Perhaps it touched my mother. Their expressed surprise cut a deep impact in her. She realised that she had never thought in that light. In fact, after the death of my father, she had forgotten the whole business of what we call living. She was alive. That she knew. But, beyond that, she had lost her sensitivity.

After the war, when the Indian prime minister Indira Gandhi facilitated the safe return of the Bangladeshi refugees to their own country, my mother insisted that she would also go along with our relatives. She would go and just have a glimpse of her village where she had left behind long back and then would come back immediately. That was what she said.

"I would just see the geese I had left behind in our pond at the backyard and then would come back," she said, at which they all burst into a loud laughter, but she didn't pay any heed to it. Rather, it made her more resolute. She said, "I'll go."

And, she went.

But, perhaps it was not so easy to come back immediately. Months went by. She would write every month that she would be returning soon. But, she didn't. Finally, she wrote to me: "It will be better if you try to come here. Your uncle says he would manage to get a job for you." In the meantime, I have been trying to go to my old village. But, here they are not taking any interest, rather discouraging me. I don't know why. Otherwise, they are so good! They are certainly going to arrange something for you. We will settle here, in our own land, once again. We will start our lives afresh!"

The very same day, towards the evening, I got a telegram. With the telegram in my hand, I was wondering what it could be about, when...

I had written up to this, when I started feeling uneasy, as if something inside was holding me back. It was a late noon hour of August. The weather was not so comfortable. There was a downpour some days back, and since then, it hadn't rained at all though clouds had been seen gathering here and there in the sky and thereby making the days more humid and clammy. So, I thought a stroll outside would be refreshing. I stirred and started walking down leisurely.

I had no idea for how long I had been walking around, but when I stopped, strangely, I could not believe what I saw before my eyes. It was an open space near a slum, a slightly developed slum, one could say. Even from a distance, one could see in the midst of some shanty, some huts with brick walls and roofs of asbestos or tin, low roofs, of course. There were even plenty of hut-like structures with walls of split bamboos and mud with roofs of different varieties of low-cost or broken tiles, dried straw, polythin sheets and worn out tarpaulin or even just a bunch of dried coconut leaves stretched on an unsteady bamboo-frame, some slanting on both sides, some sliding on one side, some almost flat with only the centre raised a little. And, almost all of those houses or huts were without windows.

I saw my onetime classmate, the refugee boy from East Bengal, who used to tell me about their family, whatever he could gather from his mother or father or from any of his relations here. I saw him on an improvised podium spiritedly addressing a gathering.

I had come to his place there twice or thrice. It was not yet a house then, just a shed, a kind of dark, unventilated shed without anything called rooms or anything of that sort. I couldn't remember though the materials the low walls were made of, but something like a roof was there, slanted and made of some pieces of mustard-oil-tin nailed together against the wooden planks of packing boxes.

It was one of those boxes that I was given to sit on when I had been to his house for the first time. It was then that I could come to know about his nickname Sontu. He was known as Santosh in the college. As we reached his place, I could hear a female voice calling out from inside the shed, "Who is it *re,* Sontuuu?"

"It's my friend, *maa.* Arun." Shouting back to his mother's query, Santosh asked me to sit on one of those boxes and went inside.

Left alone in that surrounding, I felt awkward. The front of my friend's house looked so neat, smeared with cow-dung-water, but a few yards away, it not only looked nasty with heaps of waste material along with sewage water and its stench, but the whole scene appeared extremely sickening.

Standing alone in its midst, I started feeling more uncomfortable when I became aware that I was assailed by eyes all around me, eyes expressing innocent curiosity, suspicion, incredibility, envy, dislike, fancy, fascination, and even fear! But, I was relieved of the situation with the emergence of an extremely emaciated and haggard old man from inside the shed. All the eyes suddenly withdrew, and those pairs that were still defiant were shouted away nastily, frightened more by the grimacing face of the old man than his voice.

He looked straight at me and first expressed his surprise that I was still standing. He bent over and dragged one packing box towards me while asking me repeatedly to sit on it. I could guess him to be the father of my friend, Santosh. So, I bowed to him saying *namaskar*. He felt extremely glad and telling, "Sontu is coming instantly." He humbly expressed his shame and helplessness that he had nothing else to offer me as a chair or stool so that a "gentleman's boy" like me could sit. I could get at his sentiment and so feeling ashamed of my ill-manner, I tried to manage the situation.

"No, *mousa*! It's not anything like that. It's rather, how can I sit when you remain standing?"

My friend's father seemed to be immensely pleased at that. He smiled and nodding his head in appreciation said, perhaps more to himself, "Yes, I have rightly said! A gentleman's boy! A gentleman's boy can only be so sensitive! This is what is called culture. This is what is called education!" He went on mumbling like that and then sat on a plank of plywood placed on some bricks at its ends, unrolled the fringe of his dirty lungi at the skinny waist and took out a *biri* and a dampened matchbox. Holding the *biri* in between his tightened lips, he tried to light it, trying for several times and failing each time.

"*Dhyaat*!" Throwing away the matchbox in disgust, he turned his palms upside and down alternately and said, "Do you know? *Hnaa*! What's your name after all?"

I said, "Arun."

He resumed, "*Hnaa* Arun! I was telling that this is our fate! We have been trying hard, only to live. But, to what end? Is it the way that one should live? Is it called living? Surviving. We are surviving anyway, like those pigs wallowing in dirt and filth!"

The stink was getting unbearable. Unconsciously, the back of my right palm was repeatedly moving towards my nose. Perhaps his father noticed and taking pity on me called out, "*Ore* Sontu! Where did you vanish? Leaving your friend alone here?"

It was not my friend, but perhaps his mother's voice that came in response from inside: "*Hnaa! Hnaa*! Don't make any fuss to! Going, going, Sontu is going."

He turned towards me and repeated what he was told, "*Hnaa*, Sontu is coming. His mother isn't well. Perhaps Sontu is making tea for you."

I felt embarrassed and said, "No, *mousa*! I don't need tea. In fact, I don't have any such habit. Please, ask him not to worry!"

He smiled, "No, no, it's not exactly for you. In fact, I need it. He knows it. You are just an excuse." He tried to make the situation lighter, but I was terribly disturbed thinking that I would have to have something there in that stench! Horrible! But, there was no escape. I had to, when Santosh came out and handed over a tumbler fulfill of tea to me. And, as I took the first sip holding my breath, I thanked God that it was cold and not hot. I held the tumbler in my hand and started talking with his father, and in the meantime changing his dress, Santosh emerged from his shed.

He said, "Let's go."

I was eagerly waiting for this moment. I drank the tumbler of tea in one sip and got up. It didn't escape the notice of his father, "*Arre*! It got cold!"

I said, "It's all right. Normally, I don't take hot tea."

The next time when I went to his house, the situation was a little improved. The lane was no less dingy, but I felt relieved that the heaps of garbage were not there, nor the waterlogged sewage. Instead, there were piles of cheap bricks. My friend Santosh said that his father was going to raise a room at least, a small room, with a roof of asbestos or corrugated tin.

"I am also trying to earn a bit more. I have taken up some more tuition." With a chuckling smile, he said, "You know? I am now in good terms with *Bansi* Biswal."

"Oh! The Municipal chairman?" I asked.

Santosh said: "Yes, he has a fair chance for the next Assembly election. I am working for him."

"Working, means?" I asked.

"Working as an organiser. We have formed an association here, the Destitute Association. You know how many people are there? A vote-bank that cannot be so easily ignored! And, not that all are like us, refugees from the East Bengal. There are so many homeless people here with us even from this state. And, we know what it means to be homeless!"

My next visit to his place was after a long interval. But, he used to tell me, almost regularly, the development that was going on in his slum and how it was *Bansi* Biswal who was giving them all help.

"And what about your house? Is it made pukka?" I wanted to know.

He said, "No, not exactly pukka, but at least two rooms now have brick walls." He said with a lot of satisfaction and invited me to come one day. "*Baba* would be very happy! He likes you very much."

So, I had been to his house after the final exam in the college was over. What had struck me then was the changed look of the slum. It now had the look of a habitable place though the signs of poverty, misery, sanitation and electrical problems, dirt, filth, and destitution were quite glaring. No provision for toilets, no electricity, no water facilities except a tube well at the end of the slum, attracting the attention of the strangers more by the wrangling around it rather than by its beneficial existence there.

It was then that I could come to know about my friend's political activism. He told me how he had been working actively for *Bansi* Biswal, and that whatever development I had noticed, it was because of him *Bansi* Babu. To please him, again I gave an appreciative look at the surrounding and nodded my head. His face gleamed. I took notice of his beaming face and refrained myself from making any further comment, lest he felt hurt. But, he was sharp enough to read my mind. He said, "I know you want to say something, kind of cautioning me against any adverse upshot in future. No?"

I took some time to say, "Yes."

"What is it about?" he asked.

I said, "Well, there isn't anything particular, but I think when one gets involved in such activities, one has to think of its fallout in future."

I had hardly finished my sentence when Santosh flared up, "What fallout?"

I again took time to say, "That I don't know exactly. It's only that I am having some kind of gut feeling that it might lead to some worse trouble for you."

Then, there was silence for a long time. Santosh broke the silence with a wry smile, pitying on me that I was a novice in life. "My dear friend!" he said, with an implicit sarcasm. "You have absolutely no idea about what life is. You have not yet seen the life. The realities of living."

He uttered the "seen" with such a heavy and long accent that I thought as if he was trying to inject into my vein what he had "seen," the life, as he claimed. I felt hurt, no doubt, at his snobbishness but preferred to keep myself quiet. For a moment though, I was instinctively impelled to strike him back with his own word 'seen.' *"What kind of life you have seen, my dear friend! You have seen only that which had been shown to you. Have you ever tried to see by yourself? Have you ever? Try. Try my dear friend!"*

I thought of saying it but didn't utter a word.

We were walking along silently. I knew both of us were feeling uneasy about the turn the situation took through our casual talk. I felt embarrassed at my own unspoken thought, and I was sure that my friend Santosh also must have been feeling so for hurting me, which certainly was not his intention. In fact, it was he again who broke the silence, "I'm sorry, *yaar*! I shouldn't have said so."

I immediately tried to make him free of any such guilt. "No, no," I said. "I didn't mind it. After all, anybody in your situation would do what you have been doing. And, anybody would react that way. There is nothing wrong in your reaction."

Later that day I had meals in his house. Santosh's father seemed to be extremely happy. I didn't know why he had taken so much liking for me. He could not decide how to express his happiness over my coming to his house and taking meals, sitting on the *kachha* floor, though I had been insisting that I was quite used to it, he protesting all the while "How could it be? You are a gentleman's son of an educated family. You might be having meals sitting on the floor. That is our way, not of those *latsahib babus* trying to be *bileti*." Suddenly, he would start taking his son to task. "Hey! You *latsahib babu*! Do you see? Learn! Learn from your friend! This is what is called culture!" And then, turning to me, he would carry on, "I know it's this culture in you that has made you so polite that you say you are used to it. You must have cemented floor."

I immediately said, "No, uncle, of course, now we have cemented floor, but we were having the *kachha* floor for a long time."

At which my friend's father burst into laughter. "Oh Ho! Ho! Ho! You are talking about your ancestral house in the village! That is gone!" With a long audible sigh, he suddenly stopped and then said, "It is lost forever!"

The atmosphere all of a sudden started to weigh on us. I looked at my friend. A glum face. Just for a moment, it struck me that I should say, "I am also a homeless destitute like you, uncle! I, too, can share your sentiments." It came to me just for a moment, but then I thought it would possibly hurt his sentiment more that I was unnecessarily pitying him. So, I flicked away the thought from my mind instantly and rather, perhaps, to lighten the air said, "*Masima*! Could I have a bit of more *sukto*?" It startled them all, my friend, his father, and his mother, my utterance of the name of the item with a pure Bengali accent. The next moment I watched his mother hurrying towards me with a bowl in her hands and with a gladness spread all over her face.

"*Baba*! How could you know the name of the item?"

I evaded the answer. Instead, I said, "*Masima*! I like it very much."

That was the last I had been to my friend's house.

After that we had occasionally come across each other and had some nice time talking about many things: his family, his father, mother, the house they were trying to raise, local politics, political rivalry, national and even international affairs, and a lot more. But then, as I know myself, I have little interest in such matters, matters that do not concern one's whole being perhaps I hardly find interesting, and that might be the reason why it used to be that it was practically my friend, Santosh, who would be talking all the while and I would just be giving him company with my ears pricked up.

In fact, those days were quite different in Santosh's life. He hardly had time to talk to me if ever I would happen to come across him. Even his father seemed to be extremely preoccupied with very odd engagements. Once, when I saw his father at a typing job, I felt curious. What has Santosh's father got to do with typing work? I went over to him. Seeing me there, his face beamed so brightly that it immediately struck my attention. It was like something of a surprise to me. I could not remember if I have ever seen such a face of his father. With an enormous smile spread over all his face, he came over to me and on his own said, "Sontu has given me a task to get these papers typed anyhow by the evening."

"What papers?" I asked.

"It is about the details of the shelters we are having now with names and all other details of each of our families," he said and handed over the papers to me for a glance at them. I saw the papers. It was a kind of pro forma asking the names and description of each member of the family, their age, dependent and earning member, sex, school/college going children, including the description of their respective shelters like what are they made of, materials used for walls, flooring, roof, doors, windows, etc.

"What are these for?"

His father said, with an expressed sense of satisfaction, "That, I cannot say, but I know only this much that *Biswal babu* is going to change our fate." And then, taking the papers back from me, said with an outlandish happiness shining forth on his face, "My dear son! You will see, very soon we are getting settled!"

The way he said "getting settled" had an instant effect on me. It made me sentimental. I remembered my father. All through my life perhaps, I was looking for that radiance on my father's face as I could see it then at that moment glimmering forth from the wrinkles of this old man's face! The whole scene overwhelmed me so deeply that I stood there speechless. I didn't feel like inquiring anything more about those papers or what was it for.

I remember, the whole day I spent as if under a spell. I came back home immediately without posting the application for another job I was interested in. Back home, I lay down straight on my bed, looking up at the ceiling fan. It was still not moving, since I had not switched on. The stillness of the fan always appears odd to me. If it's not moving I feel it stares at me, a frightening stare.

Towards the evening, I got up. A kind of apprehension and curiosity, both, drove me to the slum area. When I reached there, it was the dusky hour of the day. People had returned or were on their way back home. I was about to enter the dwelling places when I saw Santosh at a distance in front of a shack with his eyes on a bunch of papers, surrounded by a group of slum dwellers, mostly the children and old men. Hesitating, I stopped there. A moment after, when the crowd around him thinned out, Santosh could see me from there. He waved his hand, following which I moved forward. With a broad smile, Santosh welcomed me and said, "*Hnaa*! You've come at the right time. Could you please help me? It will be soon dark, and I can't complete the work today."

So, I had to help him. He explained to me what to do. It was, in fact, those papers which I had seen with his father. The papers had been typed out. They were in the form of questionnaires. I was simply to fill in the information as provided by the dwellers. It seemed they were all briefed about this by Santosh or his father, perhaps, because as I saw no one asking what it was about. Rather, there was a rush for the entry of their details. The dwellers were not even ready to wait for their turn to come. Sometimes a group of them would be shouting out the details of their families in chorus making it absolutely impossible to note them down. Sometimes even, physically stronger ones would try to elbow out others in a bid to get his name entered first, and that would lead to a scuffle, compelling Santosh to threaten them into silence by pretending to tear off all these papers and throw away so that "You people will go on suffering. Suffer in misery, in poverty, in destitution, eternally, eternally suffering! Understand? You rascals were born for that! Understand?" Santosh would shout at them, and then only again, the work would proceed. And, it went on repeatedly for sometime. Not that all of them were hopeful about a turn round of their fate. "It would be a magic then, if at all it happens." They talked among themselves, but that didn't deter them to scramble for enlisting their names. They were not hopeful but looking for a magic anyway.

Perhaps it was this expectation of a magic to take place that had gripped the mind of my refugee friend Santosh. By the time it was evening, the job was almost complete. When the night fell, the whole slum was submerged in darkness. There was no electricity. Those who could afford were using kerosene lanterns, but most of the houses had only either earthen lamp or a *dibi*, a small improvised kind of a base of a lantern without the glass-frame on it to protect the flame from the air to blow away. The thick darkness punctured by such weak flame coming out of the drooping shelters lent a funereal ambience to the entire slum.

Santosh and I then walked out of the slum to the main road nearby. We sat on the raised cemented cover of a culvert. Fortunately, there was moonlight. I could see the full moon, big and round, luminously hanging at the lower sky. A thin layer of silvery white was laying spread all over the Earth before us. Santosh appeared quite happy.

I asked him, "Do you really believe that Biswal *babu* is going to change your fortune?"

Santosh had no hesitation in saying, "Why not?"

"Because he is basically a politician."

Santosh said, "Yes, that is exactly why he will have to do it. We are not a very negligible vote-bank. He can't expect to win without our votes."

I said, "That is exactly the reason why I have a strong hunch about the whole goings-on."

"What hunch?" Santosh asked.

"What guarantee is there he is not going to back out once he wins the election?"

"How can he?" Santosh wondered.

"Why won't he?" I asked him.

Santosh couldn't say anything for a moment. But then, he explained to me how it was in front of him that Biswal *Babu* discussed the matter with the town-planning officer, and that it was at the officer's suggestion that the questionnaire was prepared. Once the details are ready it would be convenient for Biswal *Babu* to work it out immediately after the election.

I said, "But what makes you sure that it is Biswal *Babu* who is going to win the election?"

Pat came Santosh's reply, "That you can take for granted. I am hundred percent sure about it. How could it be otherwise when our votes are counted as the deciding factor?"

"How?"

Santosh said, "You see, I am not only mobilising this slum but all the pockets of slums and temporary dwellers of the whole area in the periphery of the town. Their number can't be ignored so easily." He said with such a strong sense of self-assurance that I didn't feel like rupturing it.

Even then, I just couldn't resist myself saying, "But you don't know the politicians in our country! One must be wary of them!"

Santosh didn't pay any heed to what I said.

That was the last when we had met before the election. During the election, I was not present in the town. When I came back, it was all over. And coming to know that Biswal *Babu* had won with a thumping majority, I got curious about my refugee friend Santosh. A couple of months had passed after the election.

That day, therefore, when my eyes suddenly ran over him addressing a gathering standing on a makeshift dais, I was not very much surprised. Rather, it was a kind of an augury that I had the hunch of. I waited long for the meeting to be over so that I would have some words with him. But, it went on and on. My friend spoke, in fact, shouted in a high pitched voice, not less than an hour or so, and what I gathered from his and others' speeches that there was brewing a trouble which at any time might lead to violence. They were trying to stir up the slum-dwellers to protest against the unjust decision of the local authority for demolishing all the unauthorised houses in those slums. The authority is going to put up a Science Park for the children.

"Whose children after all? Not ours, certainly! Children of those *babus*, of the higher class. Those children who have their comfortable houses to live in, majestic school buildings for education, and now they are to spend their leisure time and holidays! But, what about our children? What about us? As such we are rootless, destitute. Where shall we go? We are not going to budge an inch from our places, and not only that; we would rather demand for declaring us as the authorised occupants of the respective lands we have been trying over these past years to raise our shelters on. After all, could these structures be called houses? Does anybody call the pigsty a house? Won't it be a mockery of civilisation? And, how long would we go on moving from one place to another? Is it our fate? For what fault of us? And, if at all it is fate, then we will rise against that fate. We shall put up a battle against that fate, we are not going to take it lying low this time." My friend made the declaration followed by loud cheers and long clapping.

It went on with speaker after speaker repeating the same vows and determination. It was getting dark, and so I thought it would be better to talk to my friend some other day, calmly and alone, not in a crowd, or when he wouldn't be in an agitated mood.

Coming back home, I felt restless. It was exactly the hunch I had since the day Santosh broached me about his mess up in politics. In fact, I had even tried to caution him against such a development. I thought I shouldn't delay anymore to talk to him about these matters. Matters of political goings-on, that he might be trapped.

A week later, one morning, I got up quite early from the bed and went straight to Santosh's house. I knew this was the time when he would be home, or else he would go away for the private coaching he had taken up rendering to earn a little more besides his regular work as a baby food supplier to the retailers.

It was quite early in the morning. The sun was yet to rise. There could be seen only a faint glow of redness in the eastern corner of the sky. The road was empty except a few cyclists passing now and then, mostly the newspaper hawkers and the milkmen, the milk cans dangling from both the sides of the cycles producing a typical rhythmic tinkling sound as the milkmen would pass by on their cycles.

When I reached near their slum, the whole scene there took me by surprise. First, I felt intrigued. What was the date? I thought. Was it a national celebration day like the Independence or Republic Day? The entire open space under the cover of a colourful canopy looked so festive with tricolor flags and festoons all around. A public relation van was also there blaring patriotic songs. Getting curious, I asked some people hanging around there what it was all about. Most of them were either haggard old men or urchins. Either they didn't feel like answering me or just grimaced. Then, I asked a police personnel standing there. He said that the urban minister was coming to lay the foundation stone for the Children's Science Park.

I asked, "Science Park! Where? Here?"

The policeman said, "Yes, certainly here, where else?"

I said, "But, it is such a small place!"

The policeman said, "Small place! *Arre babu*! It's the entrance here. The whole slum area is marked out for the Park." The policeman said waving his hand at the slum nearby.

I was silent for some time, remembering the speech that day that my refugee friend Santosh and some other speakers were making so loudly. I got curious and so asked the policeman, "But, where will these people go?"

The police man didn't even take time to reply, "Let them go to hell! Who asked them to come here?"

"But, they don't have the place to go back."

The policeman said, "Why? Let them be back to their own places they have come from."

"That's the tragedy, sir! They have been forcibly thrown out of their own places and can't get back now."

The policeman then threatened me with express irritation, "Hey! You! You're their leader it seems! So, you're that rascal foreigner Sontu *babu*! Inciting these peace-loving people?"

The offensive manner of the policeman hurt me much. I felt insulted and so sharply retorted in English, "Look, Mr.! Simply because you are a policeman does not mean that you can take everybody for a ride! Mind your language first." The policeman was not prepared for such a retort perhaps, and so he stared at me and then turned away.

It was then that I saw a lorry stopped on the main road, and a gang of rowdy young men got down from its open backside raucously shouting victory to the minister! All of them had a typical jagged look. A boorish demeanor was explicit on their squalid dresses with a red scarf worn around the forehead. One could easily identify them as nothing but a gang of hooligans. Their leader, a tall and lanky fellow brandishing a stick, commanded them in a guttural voice to take positions at different spots of the ground and asked one group to be at the place in particular where the slum begins. The pot-bellied, skinny, famished-looking children and urchins, some naked, some in tattered pants, some with a smutty loin cloth around the groin, in bare body, with unkempt, un-oiled hair, hanging around in curiosity, got such a growling and a stern stare from the leader that they huddled together in fear.

The lanky leader, lifting the stick, shouted grumpily at them: "Hey! You! Sons of bitches! Go and sit there in front of the dais there silently!" And then pointing at an elderly looking boy called him, "Hey! You scoundrel, come here!" The boy looked scared. The lanky leader then grabbed the rickety arm of the boy and hauling him out towards the slum said with a vigorous shove, "Go! And, tell all your bloody people in the slum to be on the ground here within half an hour! Anybody seen in their bloody dens after half an hour will be flogged out to the meeting here. The minister is to address them. They can't be allowed to boycott him. Understand!" The boy nodded, trembling. The leader gave another shove and said, "Yes! Go and tell them!"

Slowly, I was getting at the thing. The slum dwellers must have decided to boycott the minister to register their protest against the proposed park there since it meant they were to be displaced. But, what seemed queer to me was Bansi Biswal's win in the election. If he won with the support of these people, how could he allow such things to take place? Moments later, from an officer sitting in the public relation van, I gathered that unfortunately Bansi Babu's party had lost in the election. The authority was now in the hands of his opponents' party. I asked the officer in the van if Bansi Babu was to address the meeting to which he almost snarled at me, "Which Bansi Babu?"

I said in a feeble voice, "Local MLA?"

At this, the officer sneered at me, "Haaaa! Does he have a locus standing?"

The officer's sneering voice made the picture clear to me.

A few minutes later the picture started to take place live before me. First, the wrinkled old faces emerging in ones and twos from the shelters and shanties started walking lazily towards the meeting spot, followed by splinter groups of people, younger in age, wrangling among themselves while moving back and forth between the slum area and the meeting ground, even the women folk, old and young, were also seen with the fringe of their crumpled, slovenly saris drooping over their faces moving hesitantly towards the place. The tall and lanky leader, giving a wry smile walked up to the old folks and strangely, welcoming them like a gentleman host said in a highly pleasing tone, "Welcome uncles! Welcome aunties!

Our minister will be here within no time. I know you are all aggrieved. Isn't it? Who doesn't have any grievance after all? Tell me. But, we need to bring it to the notice of the minister. Isn't it? But how? By boycotting him? Or, by telling him straightaway? And, you are now getting this opportunity to let him know, to talk to him personally. Isn't it?" The old folk nodded. The lanky leader commanded his group to see that they sit comfortably.

The splinter groups were still bickering among themselves, undecided. It was then that I saw my friend Santosh emerge there followed by three to four people. He was seen persuading a group not to come to the meeting spot. It seemed the young slum dwellers were not prepared to listen to Santosh. They were opposing him vehemently, by shouting and gesticulating. One of them even almost came to blows, and suddenly then, something dramatic happened. At the indication of their leader, the groups of those ruffians started shouting slogans uttering the names of the minister and the defeated opponent of Bansi *Babu*. As the slogan in favour of Bansi *Babu*'s opponent was going on more vigorously, a police van pulled in to the welcome gate of the ground, and a number of armed police jumped down from the van. At this, the situation at a distance suddenly took an ugly turn. The opposing young group tried to enter the ground defying Santosh's appeals, following which Santosh and his tiny group of supporters tried to detain them forcibly. But, finding him to be completely overpowered by his opponent group, ultimately, Santosh lay flat on the ground preventing the defiant to move forward.

Till then, the lanky leader was watching the whole drama silently. It was when Santosh prevented the people by lying on the ground that he swung himself into action. Brandishing his stick above his head, he shouted gruffly, "Hey! Hey!"

The attention of the wranglers now turned to the lanky leader majestically walking down towards them. Reaching there, he moved his roving eyes over the gathering and then flaunting his stick with a swishing swing gurgled in a guttural voice, "Hey! Who is this swine lying here?" After that hoarse utterance, he waited for sometime. There was a tense silence. Nobody moved. Nobody dared say anything even. The lanky leader took a glance around him and then stroking Santosh lying on the ground with the tip of his stick made his guttural voice louder. "Hey! You son of a bitch! Get up and get away!"

The lanky leader's behaviour enraged the followers of Santosh. They furiously shouted at him, but the lanky leader was unmoved. He turned towards the shouting people, looked sternly with his fiery eyes and then yelled, "Hey! You all sons of bitches! I say leave this place instantly or else...."

At which, Santosh's followers rushed to him. "Or else what? *Ynha*? What are you going to do? *Ynha*?"

The lanky leader, still unmoved, gave a sterner look and then swinging his stick violently gruffed, "Want to see? Like to see what I can do? Like to see?"

Just at that moment, the armed policemen swiftly getting into action rounded up the followers of Santosh and within a wink of eye lifting Santosh from the ground threw him down into the van. All the people there stood speechless. Before anybody could follow what exactly was happening, the police van with Santosh and his followers sped past the ground and disappeared from the scene.

The remaining slum dwellers then mutely walked up to the meeting ground. Sitting on the mat, they looked at each other exchanging stupid glances.

Almost after an hour, the minister reached in the midst of cheers. When the formalities and rituals of laying down the foundation stone of the science park was over with, the lighting of lamps and breaking of the coconut, the minister started addressing the gathering. He spoke about the current mantra of development which he said was impossible now without the help of modern science and technology.

"And, if at all we would like to see our nation developing, we have to see that our children are drawn more towards science. But, how is it possible? Only by tuning them up from their very early stage of education, and the science park to come up here shortly was merely a modest beginning in that direction." The minister abruptly concluded his speech with the apology that he was in a hurry to attend an important meeting with the chief minister. He drank a full glass of water and sat down on his seat when the lanky leader whispered something into the ears of a massive looking bushy person sitting next to the minister, and then that bushy person was seen whispering something to the minister. The minister looked at the lanky leader and nodding his head twice or thrice again rose to his feet. Without going to the speech desk, he took the microphone and said, "Yes! I am to make an announcement here. I had left it to your honorable local leader (pointing at that person) to do that, but since he desires and I am told that all of you also desire, so I can say this much. I can give you assurance that the authority will not be blind to the difficulties to our sons of the soil. The difficulties that might come in the way of putting up a science park here will definitely be addressed, too. I declare again that no sons of the soil will ever be deprived of his right to live on this soil."

It was not clear whether the slum dwellers felt assured or could follow the import of the minister's speech. They stayed looking at him dumbly with gaping mouths. The lanky leader started clapping violently, and then the crowd followed him hesitantly.

In the evening, I went there to see what happened to Santosh and his followers after the meeting was over, whether they were still kept detained or have been released. As I was entering the area, I saw people, mostly aged and young, too, discussing something in groups in undertones. One or two were seen doing all the talking, and the rest in the group were either simply nodding in affirmation or denial or were mere mute spectators. There was a kind of hushed atmosphere there. I couldn't spot Santosh or any of his followers. With much hesitation, going over to a group, I asked about Santosh and whether he has been released. To my query, one aged in the group upturned his lips with a shrug and didn't say anything. I again asked, "Has he been released?" But, they remained silent. I felt embarrassed. Helpless, I stayed there for a moment, and then as I turned to leave the place, one of the younger ones from the group called me back.

"Hey! *Babu*! Listen." He came forward to me and asked boorishly, "You're a friend of Santosh?"

I said meekly, "Yes."

Pointing his finger at me he warned: "Listen! *Babu*! Don't ever show your face again!"

I just innocently asked, "Why? What happened in the meantime that you people are behaving like this? I have seen you moving along with Santosh!"

The young man stared at me with a clear sign of threat, and then again pointing his finger at me said, "See! It won't be good either for you or for your friend. Is that clear?"

I didn't know what to say. I could only sense that something violent was boiling up slowly and slyly. Since it was getting dark, I thought it wouldn't be wise to linger on there any more. So, with a gesture of awkwardness, I left the place silently.

On the way then, I came across a boy heading towards the slum. I could recognise him by face. I had seen that boy in the morning trying to defend Santosh against that lanky leader. Stopping him on the way, I asked about Santosh. Looking quite excited, the boy replied, "Yes! Yes! He was released within an hour. It was just a kind of preventive action by the police, but the whole affair was prearranged by Mohini *Babu*."

I asked, "Who is this Mohini *Babu*?"

The boy expressed surprise at my ignorance, "You don't know Mohini *Babu*? Our Biswal *Babu*'s opponent?"

"But, he was defeated, wasn't he?"

"Yes, and that is the source of all troubles now. He knew that our Santosh bhai organised the whole thing so strongly that he couldn't get even a single vote from the slums anywhere in our town. And now, he is all after Santosh bhai! He knows if he can eliminate Santosh bhai, he would be sure of his win next time."

"*Hnaa*! It's quite natural, but I don't understand what the trouble is about? You slum dwellers have gathered round Santosh. How can he eliminate him?"

"*Arre Babu*! You don't know us people! Mohini *babu* is on a very dangerous move." The boy came close to me and said in a guarded voice, "He is playing a very dangerous card. He has raised the issue of foreigner. He is a very cunning fellow like the jackal, spreading the message that once those who have migrated from Pakistan are thrown out, the rest of the dwellers will be comfortably settled. Do you know who his target is?

"Yes, I can guess. It's obviously Santosh."

"Exactly!" The boy said.

"But, what is your Bansi *Babu* doing? Why is he hiding now?"

"*Arre Babu*! You don't understand this simple sum! How many of these Pakistani or Burmese refugees are there here? You can just count them on fingers! The majority is local, sons of the soil as they say."

I said, "But, what guarantee is there that majority is not going to be duped again?"

Swaying his whole body, the boy said, "*Arre Babu*! That is what stupid people like us don't understand!"

I asked, "What are you going to do then? I mean, what is Santosh thinking of?"

The boy then suddenly grew suspicious. Giving a piercing look at me he asked, "Why do you ask all these things? May I know who you are?"

Before I could say anything, he snapped, "I'm not going to tell you anything." And then, all of a sudden he turned away his face and in the blink of an eye disappeared in the darkness of the evening.

I was certain the day would come when the events would take that way as it had been happening in history. It had been happening, and it was bound to also this time. All the time. All the time. It always happens that way.

Only that way.

And, that is history.

I started feeling terribly disturbed and upset.

I felt agitated. Something was seething in me. A violent rage against history. Against the past. Against the whole business of what is called living. Against what is called the world. I was pretty sure my friend Santosh was going to meet the same fate as his own old father had met. They were sure to be displaced, dispossessed. This time also. His father's late renewal of passion for a house was sure to brew another trouble. Again violence. Again bloodshed. Again deaths. Again helpless cries fading out in the air.

The thought of my friend's imminent plight upset me and made me so emotional that in an absurd rage, I looked up and spat at the sky.

Even a couple of days after, I was still feeling restless. I thought I should go and see what happened to my refugee friend Santosh. So, one morning, I set out to his place. But, reaching there, I found that the situation had gone worse. Somehow or other, I sensed a kind of secretive air in the whole atmosphere. I passed by one or two persons and noticed that they were casting a suspicious glance at me. It made me feel a bit unnerved. But then, I thought it would be more foolish to go back from here and also felt scared about asking anybody anything. So, I just kept on walking ahead, and it was when I turned towards Santosh' shed that my eyes fell on that boy I was talking to in the evening before. He was there sitting under a *peepal* tree in a deep pensive mood, alone. But, what struck me was the bandage wrapped round his forehead. Coming close, I could even notice the streaks of blood on the bandage. Surprised, I asked, "*Arre*! What happened to you? What's the matter?"

The boy looked up at me and then immediately turned his face away with an expression of disgust. I repeated the question, but there was no answer. He stayed tight-lipped.

The whole atmosphere made me more anxious. With much worry, when I approached Santosh's house, Santosh was not home. It was his father who came out holding a piece of paper in his hand. I was stunned to see his face. The glow I had noticed on his face that day before the election, was gone. He looked completely worn out, broken, with a pale face, disheveled hair, shrunken eyes, looking almost like a phantom.

Before I asked anything, he held out the paper to me.

I saw that it was an official notice for eviction. He was asked to leave the place within fifteen days, failing which the authority would be constrained to evict him forcefully.

The situation was so embarrassing that I couldn't think of anything but to keep on standing there, speechless. Santosh's father also stood there gazing at me so helplessly that I felt extremely disconcerted. After some time, heaving a long sigh, he muttered repeatedly, "We are undone. We are undone. Where shall we go now?"

It was then that the whole scene started taking a nasty turn. As Santosh's father was mumbling "We are undone. We are undone," a swarthy elderly woman squatting nearby with a tooth-brushing twig in her mouth retorted in an undertone, "Go to hell! Who cares?"

At which, Santosh's father suddenly flared up, "Hey! You woman! What did you say? What did you say?"

Raising her head, the swarthy woman said in a more defiant tone, "You didn't hear what I said?" She paused and then, flinging the twig she was using for brushing her tooth away, said loudly, "I said go to hell! Hell! Do you hear me now?"

The tone, the gesticulation, and the words were enough to provoke the old man to a height of rage and frustration. I saw him standing silently, staring at the woman. His breath was growing faster, eyes sharp and red. He was fuming within groping for words. "You! You shifty, treacherous woman! You are telling this to me! You, Ramu's mother! I gave you the sheet of tin for your roof, and you are telling me to go to hell!"

By that time, concerned by the noise and especially of a shrill female voice, people of the neighboring houses started peeping out and then crowding round the old man, Santosh's father. There were old men and women, elderly, too, but none of them came forward to interfere. All stayed standing as silent spectators. Some naked and half-naked children even squatted down there with hands crossed on their chests to watch the whole drama in absorbed curiosity. And, in the midst of a ring of crowd, at the centre, was helplessly standing a frail old man, like a clown in a circus-ring, shouting in complete desperation,

"Look at this woman! This treacherous woman tells me to go to hell! Sending me to hell!"

Someone from the crowd mocked at the old man, "Why hell, *mousa*? Better go back to your own land."

Santosh's father was stunned. It was that young man who a couple of days back had warned me not to come here again. Santosh's old father was still looking at that boy in utter disbelief when that swarthy woman squeaked, "Yes! Yes! Go back to your own land and allow us to live in peace in our land!"

Santosh's father, the emaciated, scrawny old man, raising his hands and head up to the sky above, squealed, "*Hnaa* God! Land! Land! Our land! But, where is my land? Oh God! Tell me where my land is! Where? Where?"

Rising to the highest pitch, suddenly, the voice broke down to a shrill heart-rending cry. Slumping on the ground, slapping on the head with two palms, the old man was crying, tears rolling down on his shrunken chin.

I left the scene, unnoticed. Even reaching the main road, I could still hear the cry, so piercing, so desperate, and so helpless!

Coming back home, I felt totally blank. There was no power. I lit a candle and trying to set it somewhere on the table, I saw on the table was lying the last page of the novel I was trying to write, the incomplete part of what I was planning to end with.

With the telegram in my hands, I was wondering what it could be about, when...

The sentence was left there hanging.

In the shadowy darkness of my lonely room, I sat on a chair for a long time with my eyes on the incomplete sentence of my manuscript. Hours passed. And then, I uncapped my pen, held it in between my thumb and the forefinger, pressed it, went on drawing imaginary lines in the air, struck the pen against my skull, for a long time, but then it was only blankness that I could feel.

Throwing away the pen in irritation and slouching on my back on the cot as I closed my eyes, the old widow, the mother of my friend in the novel, stood before me.

You are not attached. You are not hooked to anything.

And, since there is nothing to be hooked to, you are free. You have the freedom to create your life, and since there is no attachment, you don't have a past, too. You have only a present, a present moment only flowing. You have the freedom to create each moment of your life.

I didn't know when I fell asleep, or if I had slept at all, but when I opened my eyes, I saw the bright sunshine coming through the window. I came out, and there was a fresh morning shining outside, and I couldn't know why a strange impulse suddenly rushed through me, a queer impulse to go on a visit to the village of the girl who loved and died in my novel years back.

I boarded the bus at around 10 o'clock. The bus was almost full. I took a seat at the back, since in the front rows there was hardly any vacant seat near the window. There was one, of course, I could spot it out immediately, and I was about to sit there, when I discovered that there happened to be the wheels of the bus under that particular row, and the reason why it was left unoccupied. The vibrations from the wheels would make the seats quite uncomfortable to sit on. On days when the bus is overcrowded, passengers have no options but to sit there. And so, as I was coming out of that row, I felt that a lady sitting facing that row glanced at me, just for a while, and immediately turned towards the man, her husband perhaps, sitting by her side and trying to make his child feel comfortable in the little space given to him. While passing by that row, I gave a casual look but couldn't clearly see the face of the lady. I took a seat in the back row and forgot all those things.

The bus had a delayed start. The conductor was anxiously looking out for some more passengers to come. He was there outside the bus, pacing up and down between the bus and the stalls nearby, smoking. After a futile waiting, he threw away the cigarette in disgust and caught the rod on the door. Placing one foot on the step at the gate and leaving the other one to dangle in the air, he shouted at the helper of the bus and pulled the string for the bell to signal the driver to start the bus. The driver growled something perhaps out of impatience, and then the bus picked up speed.

It was moving too fast perhaps to make up the delay in start. I was looking outside through the window. The passing scenes far and near looked as if they were familiar to me. And, I laughed at myself. Where was I actually going? Where to? To the people and place I had made alive in my novel that I was writing! And, moreover, when the girl had already been made to die in the novel!

Again, I laughed at myself and withdrew my eyes from outside, and it was then that looking at the couple, I thought that I knew the lady. I couldn't see her face then, but from the backside, it appeared to be quite familiar. I could recollect the face and the girl, too. She was a girl then, reading with me in the same college, I remembered. At one stage even, we came close to each other. A kind of intimate relationship was in the making when suddenly she was married off. In fact, if the lady in front was the same girl I remembered, it was then exactly the way we used to sit in the classroom of our college, she, a couple of rows away in front, and I, at the backbench facing her back. If I stood up to answer any question put to me, she would turn back and would look at my face straight. I would feel embarrassed and then either gave a wrong answer or fumbled or stood silently looking at her stupidly at which she would giggle, and that used to irk me so violently that once after the class was over I gathered courage to walk up to her and ask, "What do you think of yourself, *anhaa*?" She gave a complete innocent look, "What happened? What did I do?" I was so irritated that I couldn't say anything. For a few minutes, I stood silently and then said, "No. You didn't do anything, You simply bared your thirty-two teeth!" Okay. I threw those words at her and turned away.

The next time when I met her face to face, it was at the bus stand. I was waiting for the town bus, and I saw her coming, and as she reached near me, since that was the spot where the bus would stop, I told her, "Sorry!"

She looked at me. "Why? What did you do to feel sorry?"

It was then that I thought of teaching a lesson to such a saucy girl. I said, "No, I didn't do anything. I am sorry that I saw your bare teeth."

I said that with such a heavy accent on "bare" that she blushed. Her face turned red. She turned her eyes towards the buses coming.

After that incident, we had come across each other many times, in the corridor, in the library, in the canteen, on the way and even at the same spot in that same bus stand, but we never spoke. She would look at me and go away, sullenly. That was exactly what I did, too.

It was perhaps just before the summer vacation that one day shrugging off all my resentment against her, I walked up to her straight and said, "I am really sorry."

I said and just turned away when she called me back, "Listen! Me, too."

We looked at each other in utter surprise and amusement. Some moments passed in silence. And then, suddenly, both of us started laughing simultaneously. And loudly.

It was perhaps that we developed a kind of attachment for each other. Might not be "we," but I did. Perhaps. Perhaps, because in those days of my college life, I had neither interest nor time to see anything beyond the bare subsistence of life: food, clothing, and shelter. Food and clothing we were having, minimal though, that my hapless father could manage to arrange. So, I had to take to rendering private coaching to small children to meet the expenses of my study. That was mostly in the evening hours or on Sunday mornings. It not only consumed my time, but even, I used to think sometimes that it dulled all my senses. At the end of the day, after the night meals, I used to feel so drained out that life would appear as a vast stretch of vacuum, a meaningless void. And then, an unspeakable terror, a sense of dread would grip me.

Sometimes, in order to ward off this sense of dread, I would lie down on my belly on the floor and start scribbling, nothing in particular, a sentimental poem or a pulpy prose-piece suffused with anger against God, fate, history, nation, and so many such other things. It would be painful to lie down on the belly on a bare floor.

The comfort of sleep I had never experienced. In fact, it was a kind of developed shanty that we were living in then.

So, I felt totally embarrassed and surprised when one day that girl of my class came to my house. I was not home then. My mother was worried what to speak, where to ask her to sit. As I entered and was just at the door, in astonishment, she herself started explaining that since she was absent for such a long time that she wanted my notes to make up her study and that there was no one else she could think of staying nearby, and that was why she had to come to my place. But, before I could say that she was absent in the college only for a day or two, she said, "I have got those notes. It was here, isn't it? This will do. I'll return it tomorrow in the college." Before we could make out anything, she stooped down to touch the feet of my mother saying "*Mousi*! I'll come again," and then hurriedly went out.

I couldn't decide what to do. I stood there still, and then my mother asked me to lead her up to the main road. When I came out, I was surprised that she was in fact waiting for me. As I reached her, she said, "Know? I might not be attending the college anymore."

I asked, "Why?"

She said, "My parents are arranging for my marriage." She paused, gave a thorough look at me, I couldn't know why, and then said, "They had come to see me yesterday."

Without thinking of anything, I asked, "Who?"

She looked away and said, "They. His parents and one of his friends."

I said, "*Achha, achha* (well, well), when?"

She said with a clear sign of irritation, "Told *na*, yesterday."

I said, "No, I mean, when is your marriage?"

There was casualness in my tone. To my question, she didn't say anything. Just gave me a very hard look, and then she hurried away, silently.

It was really difficult for me to understand her look that evening, or her coming to my place, or the whole thing, in fact, the thing that normally goes by the name of love, or something of the sort. Was it something called love?

In those days the waves on my mind were of different

kind. If sometimes there were waves of anger and frustration at the fated situation of my life, at the unspeakable misery, at the tiring hardships, at other times it was a kind of obsession for a lost kinship, intimacy, home, village life, and a passionate sense of belonging. A fleeting romance or a lucid, undemanding, juvenile fancy was not the material that could exert any impact on me.

My craving was perhaps for a solid, strong, vigorous, and a robust bond. Perhaps that girl had failed to send such waves to me. That was why perhaps it was only after a week or so of that incident in my house I noticed that the girl was not really coming to the college. The moment I noticed her regular absence, a kind of frustrating sensation ran through me. I didn't know why I desperately went on looking for her in every corner of our college, for days, without letting anybody mark it.

Finally, I came to know that she had been married off.

It was her face; now I could clearly recognise when rising from the seat along with her husband and the child she headed towards the door of the bus to get down. As she was stepping down, she threw a fleeting glance at me once again, just for a fraction of a second. She had changed a lot. Her slim girlish body had become hefty, and her taut face now looked so flabby. The reason why it took time for me to recognise. And, the moment I could recollect the face, a strange feeling seized me, the queer feeling of a romance that was missed, a wonderful relationship that was nipped in the bud by my own indifference.

That fleeting glance sent me almost into a trance. The bus was moving on, I was looking through the window, but it was just that only my eyes were open, the mind was completely vacant. I was lost in a trance when the bus stopped with a sudden jerk, and the jerk brought me back to my consciousness. I saw the passengers in front were craning out their heads through the windows.

There was an accident on the road. What caught my attention was a long streak of blood running down the empty space between the legs of the people gathered there. A car was lying overturned on the side of the road that I could see from the melee. When I got down from the bus, people were talking about a child who had miraculously escaped and whose parents were lying dead in a pool of blood. Some local youth had dragged the bodies out of the damaged car and were waiting for the police or a vehicle to take them to the nearby hospital though everybody present had no doubt that the couple was already dead. That was why they were waiting for the police to come and take over the matter. The crowd was talking about the child, sitting mute by the side of the dead bodies, perhaps his parents. He was neither crying nor shouting nor even looking at the people there, not responding to any of the questions or queries. He was simply sitting there, blankly, dumbstruck.

I tried to push my way to the spot to have a look at what exactly was the matter. The moment I could reach the spot, a police jeep pulled in there. The police personnel jumped off the vehicle and immediately cordoned the place preventing us to have a clear vision of the incident. One police officer was seen making a passing private car stop there. The dead bodies were being carried over to the car while the other officer was trying to talk to the child, the lone survivor. But, the child wouldn't open his mouth. With no response from the child, the police officer now started coaxing him to accompany them, but the child was stubbornly resisting.

The officer now turned towards the crowd helplessly, and then I could see the face of the child and his eyes also fell on me. Before I could comprehend anything, the child suddenly rushed to me crying "Uncle! Uncle!" He clung to me holding me tightly, like a man catching at a straw while getting drowned in a stream.

The whole scene was so stupefying that I stood there for sometime, motionless. The officer asked me something, but I could simply mumble. When I came to my senses, I couldn't know what to speak or what to do. The child was the one I had once left crying, a couple of years back.

Ultimately, it so happened that I had to bring the child with me. It was a terrible time for both me and the police personnel in the police station. The police people asked me there on the spot in what way I was related to the child. I tried to explain to them that I was not his relation in any way, and that I knew only his parents and none else. But, looking at the way the child kept clinging to me, they didn't seem to be convinced. The trouble started for me when the police people asked me repeatedly where I was going, and if at all I had any information about the child's family moving that way in a car. I denied the fact but failed to give them any clear information about my journey in the bus since I myself had no idea about why exactly I was journeying in that bus and again, if at all, I would have told them about my sudden impulse to see the village of the girl who had committed suicide years back in my novel. I would have lodged myself in a precarious zone of fiction and reality. In response to their enquiries about my bus-journey or destination therefore, I could simply mumble, and that was exactly what prompted them to be suspicious of me. I sensed it strongly when they asked me to accompany them, along with the child, to the place where I was staying, as I told them, as the child's neighbour. What was most humiliating about it was that I was not allowed to go there on my own. I was forced to sit at the backside of the police van along with the child. The inside of the van was so stuffy that I felt suffocated. There was no provision for ventilation at the backside of the van. There was only one small opening that was again wire-netted.

I was being treated as an accused suspect! Not a generous person offering his help to the police! I wondered!

Sometimes I feel that one is simply to wonder at what is going on in his life. Trying to understand is to invite irritable pain. When the police people asked me to board the van, I wanted to know if it was necessary for me to accompany them. After all, I had given them the address of the child's parents. First, the inspector said that since the child was to be handed over to his relations and that he was not prepared to go with them, it was therefore obviously necessary for me to accompany. So, I felt glad that after all I was of some help to the society, and specifically to the child for whom once I had developed a strong affection, and not only that, even I was extremely grateful to the child for the way he had changed my relationship with the world around.

But, later, I started feeling frustrated when it became clear to me that the police people looked upon the accident as an act of conspiracy and that I might be the conspirator. On our way to the child's place, the van halted somewhere, and we were asked to get down for lunch. It was there in the hotel that the inspector started asking me, "Look, Mr.! You are not sure exactly where you were going in that bus. Isn't it?" I just looked at him blankly. So, he said with a chuckle, "But, you had given a destination to the conductor, as per the ticket you showed us." I took some time even to mumble something. But, the inspector didn't pay any heed to it. He gave a stern look at me and said, "Look, Mr! We had made enquiry about that village and our inquiry had revealed that…" The inspector paused and raising his round shaped head from the rice plate gave a hard look at me and continued, "There is no any village by that name anywhere near the railway station where you had requested the conductor to allow you to get down. The bus you were traveling in normally doesn't stop there, near that station. Right?" He asked. I nodded my head without knowing what for. The inspector then lowered his round shaped head toward the rice plate before him and focused on gulping a mouthful of rice with a noisy sucking of the spiced chicken juice simultaneously. He took some time to relish the juice sweeping his tongue all over the palate of the mouth and then licking the lips outside the mouth and then looking straight at me said, "So, you were deliberately trying to mislead the police. Right?" This time I could neither nod my head nor could I make a plain answer. My eyes could only reflect a dazed look.

It was my silence that betrayed me, and the stubborn silence of the child deepened the crisis. On reaching the child's place, the police people made an intensive enquiry, with the help of the local police, about the veracity of my statement from the neighbours of the child's parents where I was also staying, and then from my former office there, and when the police people entered there, I was greeted with loud cheers and joy and my former colleagues in the office were shocked to learn about my unfortunate entanglement with the situation. My former boss even got so enraged at the whole affair that he started banging the police people for unnecessarily becoming suspicious of me, and even he warned referring to the names of his relations in the higher ranks of the police administration that he wouldn't spare them, if I was going to be harassed any further and that, too, as a return to the kind of help I had been offering to the police and to the child!

Ultimately, it worked. I noticed that after coming out of my former office the police people started behaving with me in a different tone. On collecting information about the native place of the child's dead father when they proceeded towards that place to hand over the child to his grandfather, they asked me to sit in the front along with the inspector. And, surprises were there for both of us, the policemen and me. The child was persistent on refusing to go to his grandmother or to any of his relations. To all kinds of cajoling, he maintained a mysteriously stony silence. There was absolutely no expression on his face. He stayed clung to me physically, clutching tightly at my trouser. So, there was no other way but to bring him back with me. The policemen were in a hurry to leave the place, and so without wasting any more time, they got some papers signed by the child's grandfather and me to the effect that under a strange situation the child was put under my care.

In-care-of then became my only identity since the day I had to bring the child along with me. I was then staying alone, and hence it became a stupendous task for me to take care of the child. Not that he was a bother for me. That was what appeared surprising. Abnormal. He would never disturb me, if I would be doing anything seriously. He would never be pestering or whining. And, what most perturbed me was his obeisance. It made me wary. I took him to a psychiatrist for a check-up and told the whole story. The doctor gave a patient hearing and then asked the child, "Beta! What is your father's name?" The child sat motionless, with a stony face. The doctor asked, "Where is your father, beta?" There was no expression on the child's face, sitting mum. But, when the doctor asked, "Where is your uncle, beta?" The child smiled and, swaying his whole body in amusement, pointed his finger at me. The doctor said "Ah! He is your uncle?" The child nodded his head, smiling. "What is your uncle's name?" The doctor asked. The child had no hesitation to tell my name. And still smiling.

The doctor then asked me not to worry much and advised me that it would be better to take the child as absolutely normal and also suggested to start sending him to school.

It was there at the school that I faced the real problem. The headmistress refused to admit the child unless the parents turned up. I told the whole story. She wanted to know my relationship with the child. And, when I told that I had no relationship with the child, she was stunned. She threatened me that she could call the police, but since that would be a bad scene in the school, she was not doing it.

The next day, again, I went to the school along with the doctor. That was what the doctor suggested when yesterday coming back from the school I went straight to him and told him all my problems. The doctor heard me patiently, and then asked if I had all those papers with me that the police people had got signed by the child's grandfather. I nodded my head.

"Well," the doctor said, "I will accompany you tomorrow." And that was how we met the headmistress. She first fumed when she saw me entering her office along with the child and the doctor.

"Oh! You have come again! I told you yesterday. I can't take the child without his natural or legal guardian."

Before I could say anything, the doctor pulled a chair himself. Sitting comfortably, he said, "Madam! I am a doctor, and the child is under my treatment. It was me who had advised him to send the child to a school. It is a very vital process of treatment for the child. The child had suffered a terrible trauma, and it is the only practical way that he would be able to get rid of the traumatic experience."

The headmistress listened to the doctor and then taking some time said, "Well, doctor! I understand the problem. I have all sympathy for the child, but then..."

Before she could complete her sentence, the doctor snatched the words, "Yes, madam! But then, there are certain official procedures that we normally don't want to meddle with. Isn't it?"

The headmistress smiled this time. The doctor then resumed, "If you don't mind, madam... you see, as a doctor I was not supposed to come to the school for my patient. It was rather I should have confined my treatment to my clinic only, isn't it?" The headmistress nodded her head. The doctor said, "I came, because I felt that I must act as per the need of the treatment and not according to normal medical procedures. But anyway, madam, we are not going to put you in trouble. He has with him all the police documents in respect of the child. You can see and keep a copy of all these papers. Even you can forward information to the local police along with these papers. And moreover, if you want, I myself can put my signature as a witness. I am a registered doctor."

The headmistress thought for a while and then said, "Well, I think I can take the child, but..." she looked at me and said, "Why don't you adopt the child legally?"

I couldn't know immediately what exactly to say. But then, coming back from the school feeling happy that the child could now have a normal way of life, a thought came to my mind: What difference does it make if I adopt the child legally except the fact that it would give an identity to our relationship? It would define our relationship. That he belongs to me. That the child is related to me, legally, of course, not otherwise, as a child is related to his father. That's all. How is it going to affect our relationship in real sense of the term? Is he going to eat with me more comfortably? Will the bath that he takes be more pleasing? Is it that my house is going to exude a deeper sense of intimacy? Is it that relationship depends only on a social or legal stamp? Can't there be a relationship, a belonging as it is? In its essence? Where does the river lie? In its water? Or, in it's flowing?

Normally, it is this state of mind in me that takes me to my writing table. I passionately feel like talking to someone in such unbearable moments. But, I find none around me. At least to talk about thoughts like these. Sometimes, I wonder what it is for that I do feel like this. I do think like this!

I felt restless throughout the day, and after the night meals when the child went to sleep, I took out the manuscript of the novel I was writing, lying crumpled under my bed for a pretty long time.

I resumed from where I had left.

With the telegram in my hand, I was wondering what it could be about...

When the child turned the side and as he turned in his sleep, his hand hit my right elbow at which the pen went out of my hold. I sat up to a comfortable position, and as I was sitting comfortably, my eyes fell on the sleeping child. The innocent face struck me. It was all contentment. A contentment ensuing from a sense of security.

I kept looking at his face. I didn't know for how long! And, as I was looking at, I was wondering more and more, with the pen dangling from my fingers, about my novel that I was writing and my life, my personal life that I was living. Which one was my novel? And, which one was my life? What about the child? Acting on the words of my intimate friend, I had once included the child in my novel.

What would I do now that the child had already come out of the novel and had entered into my personal life again?

As the days went by, I started discovering myself in a more bizarre state.

Around a month later, when I was waiting at the school-gate for the child to take him back home, I saw at a distance a lady was looking at me, and the moment I tried to know who it was, she turned her face away. At that very moment, the ringing of the school-bell made all of us alert to keep our eyes fixed on the children coming out of the classrooms and racing towards the gate.

Holding the forefinger of the child then, I had my eyes rolling on the swarming crowd of parents and their children trying to spot that lady but couldn't. Was it that lady in the bus stealing a look at me? That college girl, my classmate, once coming to my house mysteriously and trying to speak out her love fumblingly? Was it she?

I kept on guessing throughout the day and the night. Lying on the cot, I tried to recollect that evening the girl who had come to my house. I could recollect a face. An anxiety-ridden, worried face hardly visible under the dim streetlight, the cool evening breeze stirring hushed emotions, a pair of mysterious eyes accruing beauty from unspoken sadness...

Could it be called love? Or passion? Or one body calling another body? Is it what is called attachment? How does it originate? What is it for?

Feeling terribly disturbed I sat up on the bed, and then I saw the child in deep sleep by my side. Suddenly, I didn't know why a strange thought seized me, a thought that led me to visualise: A knock on the door. I opened the door and there was the old man standing, the child's grandfather, who said, I am to take back the child. As his grandfather uttered the words, the child woke up and appeared at the door, The grandfather stretched out his arms, said come, and the child went away with his grandfather, silently, without looking back at me, even once.

How would I take that situation? What would be my feeling? A total indifference? Nothing has happened. Or rather, something happened but doesn't matter. The sun rises and sets. The day comes and goes. Leaves come to trees, turn yellow, and fall. Clouds gather in the sky, in monsoons, downpour, and then disappear behind the autumnal blue sky, and then the cold wind blows from the north, the shine of the blue fades into the foggy winter chilling the earth that then blossoms out again with colours and vibrancy of a cheerful air.

And so, it goes on happening. How does it matter to us?

But, if the child goes away like that, silently, without even looking back at me, I felt that it would hurt me terribly. I would be entirely broken. Crippled emotionally. I can't live. I can't live! And, why should I live at all? What for?

I was struck by my own question.

The window in front was open. Sitting on my bed, puzzled, disturbed and restless, in the darkness of the night, I looked out through the window.

There was pitch-darkness outside. Nothing was visible. The whole earth was under the cover of darkness. But, it seemed, as if I could see the outline of a face, emerging out of that darkness - a sharp pair of eyes - almost burning - of my refugee friend. A gaping mouth with a row of white teeth shining like a sharp knife - with the same question: What for? We are going to be dispossessed of our land, of our house, and we have to live! How? What for? Tell me. Our houses are snatched away from us, demolished, razed to the ground, and we are to live peacefully? How? Why should we live at all then? And live where, after all? Tell me.

It was my refugee friend, Santosh, who spat out those words on me when days before, I rushed to the police station to bail him out. It was when I had been to the market I overheard people talking about the tension on the outskirt of the town. I asked what it was for. They said perhaps it was due to the eviction.

"Eviction? Why? Where?"

They told that they were not sure, but the area they described clearly pointed at the slum area of my friend Santosh. I felt apprehensive, and without going for shopping, I rushed to the place.

Reaching the place, I caught sight of a giant bulldozer with a driver on it nonchalantly watching the scene below. There was a scuffle going on between a group of agitated slum dwellers and Santosh. His father was also there. I could see him gesticulating and hotly arguing with the crowd around him. But, the crowd around him seemed to be shouting at him more fiercely. One of them, perhaps to provoke Santosh, shouted spitefully, "Hey! You brother-in-law old man! You outsider! Bloody scum! Why don't you go back to your land and leave us in peace?"

The insult to his father was too much for Santosh to stomach. He got so enraged that in his fury he forgot his precarious situation. Raising his hand, he was about to strike that man when the whole group surrounding him struck him back with violent blows and kicks. Even they didn't spare his old father which set Santosh on a brutal aggression. Lying on the ground, he managed to pick up a sharp piece of stone and flung it at the people in the fray which hit a tall man there, and he started bleeding. The sight of blood sparked off violence. The mob went furious. I couldn't understand how within no time a lot f hooligans emerging from nowhere joined them shouting: "Hey! Hey! What do these bloody swine think of them? *Ynha*? Bloody foreigners! Out to kill us! Us! And on our own land! Don't spare them! Don't! Throw them out! Burn their houses! Burn! Burn!"

Madly shouting slogans to oust the foreigners from the land, the whole mob headed towards Santosh's house. Santosh's father ran after them frantically trying to hold them back but was vigorously shoved back. He fell flat on the ground.

I was thinking of going to help Santosh when a police jeep reached the spot. The police officer had a talk with the bulldozer men and some other spectators standing there. Asking a constable to pick up the injured Santosh and to put him in the jeep, the police inspector, along with his troop, moved towards the slum. But, by that time, I could see smoke rising from inside the slum and mad shouting could still be heard piercing through empty air.

I met Santosh at the police station. He was arrested for trying to murder a slum dweller when that person was trying to persuade him to allow the authority to carry out the eviction order. That was the criminal charge against him.

He looked so furious, blood-stained face with white bandages on his head, shoulder, and cheeks, fuming and breathing heavily and noisily. Seeing me there in the police station, he gave me a stern look with a tightened fist, trying to resist my very presence there and perhaps an ugly outburst of his seething anger, too. But still, when I persisted, he started shouting at me, "Hey! You son of the gentleman! Why have you come here? To see the fun? *Yanh*? Why? Why? Why have you come here?" He couldn't speak out anything, started gasping. His whole body was throbbing; quite visibly.

It was obvious that he was trying to suppress the outburst of a violent rage that was burning him within.

I stood there silently, letting him release all his horrid emotions.

After a long silence, as he was slowly coming back to a normal state of mind, I gestured the policeman there to give him a glass of water. He didn't refuse, when offered. Rather, he sucked up the full glass of water in a breath. It was only then that I could speak to him. "Santosh! Now that you have calmed down, you can understand why I have come." He nodded his head and looked at me, vacantly. I said, "I had talked to the officer in charge here. I will bail you out..."

"No!" He flared up before I could complete my words. "Don't do it. I don't want any more mercy!"

"But I haven't come to show any mercy, dear! And moreover, who am I to do it?"

"Then, what is it for you have come?"

"That also, I don't know. But, the moment I heard about the situation, I thought I should come to help you out. I have to."

"But why? What for?" He shouted at me.

I said, "I told you *na*. I do not know why. I do the thing the way I have been doing. That's all. No reasons. No whys. I never bother for reasons, never give a damn to whys. I have come to bail you out. That's it."

I stood in silence. I had nothing more to say. In fact, I always find myself at a loss for words in such situations. As a matter of fact, sometimes even I wonder at the way we go on wasting our energy in babbling. When an immediate action is to be carried out, what's the meaning in groping for words? Words cannot substitute actions!

Silence prolonged and there was no response from my friend. I said, "So, you won't like to come out?" Turning his face away, my friend persisted on shaking his head negatively.

I waited for some time and then left the place silently.

Another stubborn child! A sulking child! Is it the way to express one's anger? Hatred? Rage? I mumbled to myself. Yes, my friend! I understand your plight. And that pains me! My dear! I feel pained! And till I see you coming out of this plight, I will myself be writhing in pain. And that's the misery, my dear!

The stubborn and violent face of my friend stayed put in my mind. I knew what he needed at the moment was to be free from the raging anger. It was not so much the police brutality as the turn of the local politics and the betrayal of the people that had crushed him badly. It was grating him inside. It was exactly that hunch that I had the day he told me about his mess up in politics months back. I could well guess that Bansi *babu* was interested in politics of vote only, and that once he won the election, he would be nobody's man. That was against what I tried to warn my friend that day, and even I had also told him that Bansi *babu*'s rival would not let the matter go so smoothly. He won't dither to strike back after the election, and in that case, as the principal leader, he would have to bear the brunt.

The next day again I took another attempt to make Santosh calm down and come to terns with reality. But again, all went in vain. Again a stubborn refusal. An unbending "No! No, I won't!"

"But why?" I insisted.

"What am I to do out there? Get another flogging! Another spank! From another bastard! Bitch!" Santosh went on gushing out venomously and then spat on the floor, literally. *Thooooh! Thooooh! Thooooh!*

I felt terribly upset that day. The whole situation made me so restive that I couldn't sleep.

I was so absorbed in my thoughts that I had not noticed that the child was still sleeping and that it was getting late for the school. I tried to wake him up. In his sleep, the child looked so innocent that I didn't feel like disturbing him. Perhaps, that was the only spot now, the child's face, where one could find the untainted picture of innocence. It was more urgent than the school. I thought.

So, leaving the child in sleep, I came out, did my morning chores, and when I entered the room, the child was sitting on the bed, drooping. At the sound of my footsteps, he raised his head and endeared in a weak voice, "Uncle, I don't feel like going to school today."

It looked so unusual, the way he was sitting, the voice, so feeble, the drowsy eyes. The whole appearance smacked of illness. I immediately went to him and placed my palm on his forehead. It was a mild fever I felt. Not to be so worried. But, the next moment a kind of strange anxiety seized me. After all, I was the only person to look after the child. No one else was there for him. It was only me that he would look up to at the time of his need.

I had never handled a child alone and so felt panicky. I had no idea about whether it was a common cold or something serious demanding immediate attention. Should I go to a doctor?

I was in a dilemma though, but I thought I should. I was his only shelter. So, immediately, I got ready to see the doctor, the psychiatrist treating him.

When I was locking the door, the child asked, "We aren't going to school, uncle?" I looked at him. A pale face. It frightened me. Lifting him to my arms I said, "No, my son."

"Where are we going then?" he asked in a weak voice.

"You know that doctor uncle? We are going to his house."

"Why are you going to the doctor uncle?" he asked.

"Why? You don't like him?"

"No, I like him, but why are we going to him?"

"Nothing, just that we won't go to school today. Rather we would have some fun with our doctor uncle in his house. Isn't he a nice man?"

"Yes, he is nice, but uncle, would he play with us?"

"*Hnaa*, certainly! He would play with us."

"No, he won't." The child said.

"Why?" I asked

"He is a big man. He won't play with a child like me."

"Why do you think so? Doesn't he play with his own kid?" I asked.

"Does he have a child? Like me? Uncle, uncle, would he play with me?" The child brought his face close to me and asked.

I said, "He would, my son!"

"Sure, uncle, he would play with me?"

"Of course, why not?"

"He doesn't know me."

"So what? He would come to know you."

"How come?"

"The moment you start playing with him."

"But, uncle, if I play and he don't?"

"You make him play."

"How long will it take to make him play?"

"So long as he doesn't come forward."

"But how long?"

"So long as he doesn't come forward."

"And, if it gets evening?'

"Doesn't matter. You go on trying."

"And, uncle, what you will be doing then? Sitting idly?"

"No, I will leave you with him in the doctor uncle's house, and..."

The child immediately held me tight and placing his little face against my cheek urged, "No, no, you can't leave me like that. You can't go anywhere leaving me alone."

Just then, I heard some feminine voice calling me from behind: "Listen! Please!" I turned back and saw the same lady. In fact, I could recognise the face now clearly. It was the same girl in my college.

By the time she came near me, the child was still holding me tightly and urging me not to leave him alone. She asked, "Your son missed the school today? I was looking for...I mean...I was wondering why the child isn't seen today...in fact, I wasn't exactly wondering but...just thinking...in fact, my son is also in his class."

I smiled and asked my child to wish her.

The child wished her a clumsy good morning in a weak

voice and again started repeating, "You won't leave me alone?"

She stroked the cheek of the child saying, "Fond of the father, *na*? He looks sick. Is he ill?"

I said, "Yes, taking him to the doctor."

"Which doctor?"

I told the name of the doctor.

She said, "He is not a pediatrician. He is a psychiatrist."

"I know, but he is the only doctor whom I know personally."

She said, "But, he isn't here in the town today. He has gone to Delhi."

I stopped. "Are you sure?"

"Yes, very much. He is a relation of mine."

I stood silently. Felt hopeless. I could take the child straight to the Government Hospital, but then I didn't have trust in those hospitals. And, I didn't have any idea about another doctor there. And, moreover, I was looking for a doctor with whom I could trust my child.

Appreciating my situation, she said, "It seems you have no idea about any doctor nearby? Perhaps the baby was born in your in-law's place?"

I tried to evade the matter and so said: "I have never before had the need of it."

She said, "Well, I can help you then, if you like."

I instantly grabbed the offer. "Please, I will be extremely grateful to you."

I noticed she blushed and said, "*Arre*! Why do you take it that way? There is nothing to be grateful. I know a child specialist, personally." She added, "Intimately, quite intimate to me." She said and glanced at me with a bit of mischievous look.

It didn't escape my notice. But then, I had become so worried about the child that I preferred not to heed it. And so, I said, "I would really be grateful if you take me to him, if you don't mind, or you can just give me the direction."

She stopped me, waving her hand. "No need to be grateful. You just come along with me."

As I followed her, the child asked, "We aren't going to the doctor uncle?"

I said, "No, my son. We would go to another place."

"Some other doctor uncle?"

"Yes, my son."

"And, this doctor uncle has a child?"

"Sure, he must be," I said.

"And the child would play with me?"

"*Hnaa*! Sure. Why not?"

"And, I won't have to make him play like the other doctor uncle's child?"

She interrupted, "Oh, he plays with his kid, *na*?"

I tried to evade again and said, "Not exactly, I would rather tell you afterwards, some other day, if at all we happen to come across again."

"All right. If at all we happen to meet again," she said with a heavy accent on "happen to" and chuckled. Took some time. And then, asked me straight, "Perhaps you couldn't recognise me?"

By that time, my anxiety had gone down. I smiled and said, "Sorry."

Throwing a surprised look at me, she repeated, "Don't recognise me?"

I said again, with a smile, "Sorry."

Her face went pale.

I said, "Sorry! I mean, we were sorry!"

She was silent for some moments and then burst out laughing loudly, saying, "Oh! You remember everything!"

The child, looking at her laughter for sometime, whispered into my ear, "Why is aunty laughing like that?"

I said, "Aunty is laughing, why? Aunty is laughing that when you will go to her place you will also laugh and play with her child, my son."

"Where is auntie's child?"

"He is in school now, my dear. In your school, in your class."

"If he is in my class, why don't he play with me?"

"It might be because he doesn't know you yet."

"When he will know me, he will be playing with me?"

"Of course. Sure," she said.

"When will he know me?"

"Any day."

"Today?" the child asked eagerly.

"Yes, today. You do one thing. You stay back in our house, and in the meantime, my son would be back, so that both of you would play together," she said.

The child looked very happy, nodded his head, and then whispered, "Would you stay back in auntie's house?"

She enquired, "What does he say?"

I said, "He wants me to stay with him, also."

She joked, "*Hnaa*! Fond of the father only na? Stupid child! Forgetting the mother altogether!"

Suddenly the child's face changed. He looked glum. I felt anxious.

She also noticed it, but took it other way: "I am sorry. He felt hurt, *na*?" She then started cajoling him, "Oh my little cute! Sulking! *Yyhna*? No, no, my child, I was just joking. You love your mother, too. You are so dear to your mother."

Getting stiff, the child turned away his face from her.

By that time, we had already reached the place, for I saw her opening the gate and asking me to follow her.

She pressed the call bell. A maidservant opened the door. She entered the room, as if her own, asked the maidservant if the sahib had already taken his breakfast, and to tell the sahib that someone was waiting for him with a child. Asking me to sit comfortably, she went inside.

I had to sit there in the drawing room for a long time. I was attracted by a photograph on the wall. It had the look of a saint. A smiling face, with a beard and long hair. It seemed as if he was looking at me and smiling. In the meantime, the maidservant came with tea and a glass of Horlicks for the child. I was wondering if it was her own house, or of a personal relation when a tall, handsome young man entered the room and welcoming me as though he was welcoming his guest very politely expressed his regret for making me wait. I felt so stupefied that I couldn't say anything. He said, "You are Neena's classmate? Happy to meet you."

I expressed my surprise, "Neena?"

The doctor felt embarrassed, "Oh, I have no idea if

she had any other name in her college. But, that's the name we know her by."

He looked at the child and asked, "Yes, what's the problem?"

I said, "No. Nothing so serious. A mild fever, I suppose."

The doctor smiled at me and said, "I see. You have already diagnosed!"

I blushed. And, it was just then that she appeared at the door saying, "*Hnaa,* its mild fever now! But, how worried he was on the way when I happened to come across him you don't know." She came straight and sat beside the doctor.

Now, I thought, I was getting at the situation clearly. The doctor was her husband, the reason why she said "intimate" with a chuckle then.

The doctor turned to her and asked, "You haven't told me about your friend earlier?"

I tried to save her from embarrassment, "No, in fact, we were just classmates...I mean...we just were known faces."

Her husband then said, "I see! In that case, you might not be knowing about our marriage? How we got married?"

She placed her hand on his mouth and shut him up saying: "No, no, don't...don't."

Her husband started laughing, trying to remove her hand from his mouth, "Well! Well! I am not telling anything."

She said, "You first take care of the child. He is sick."

"Sick? Who says?" He lifted the child to his own lap and examining him thoroughly patted on his back, "Fit! Absolutely fit! Only a bit of cold." Placing him on the sofa by his side, he took out his pad and asked, "*Beta*! What's your name?" The child told his name, and when the doctor asked pointing at me, "*Beta*! Tell me your father's name?" The child kept mum. I immediately said my name, and the child shouted, "No. No."

They were surprised at the sudden outburst of the child. His voice sounded so unnatural that even I felt embarrassed. I mumbled, "No. in fact, he addresses me as uncle and so..."

The doctor looked at the child and said: "Oh! Your uncle's name? Not father's?

The child grinned.

She said, "Funny!" Turning towards the child, she said, "Hey! You naughty! You have changed your father to uncle?"

Pulling on a long face, the child said gravely, "No, not my father. My uncle."

Her husband asked me, "Your own son?"

I thought it wouldn't be proper to tell them anything in the presence of the child, so I didn't say anything.

She said, "On the way also, I asked about his mother, and he reacted...he turned away his face."

I said, "Yes," and then couldn't speak out anything.

She said, "You say your own son, and the child is reacting strongly at the mention of father or mother. What's the matter?"

I remained silent. Suddenly then she asked, "Your wife doesn't stay with you?"

I still kept on looking blankly at them thinking what to say when she asked, "Is it the other way? You don't stay with her?"

This time I said, "I am not married."

There fell a silence. The doctor looked at me with a clear sense of curiosity, and his wife, my classmate, gave me a glance that expressed more a sense of disapproval than curiosity. I could read the sign in her look. She had taken my behaviour as unbecoming of a normal social life. Perhaps she had questions about my moral conduct also.

I imagined it must have also pained her to see her one time love falling in her esteem!

I desperately wanted to explain the situation, but then I had started feeling uncomfortable for the fact that all such talks would affect the child's mental state. The psychiatric doctor had warned me not to talk about his parents in the presence of the child. So, I had no other way but to remain silent. I could guess my silence had a different impact on them, for I marked slowly the cordial air in the room was changing. Sooner I leave the place, the better, I thought, and so getting up from the sofa abruptly, I asked, "Well! How much...I mean the fee?" I was surprised at the rudeness of my own tone.

But, it seemed, the doctor sahib wanted to make the situation lighter. Turning towards his wife he said, "Now I am convinced he is just your classmate, not a friend. Otherwise he wouldn't have talked about fee, isn't it?"

She didn't say anything, didn't even smile also. Everybody was perhaps feeling awkward and didn't know what to say.

When I came out of their house, I didn't fail to notice a kind of indifference in their behaviour. There was a marked absence of warmth that was so explicit when we entered the house. As I was getting down, the veranda the child said: "Uncle! I won't play with auntie's son?" Hurriedly trying to distract him, I said, "Yes! Yes! Sometime later. Not now. He is in the school *na*!" But, he went on insisting: "No! You said you will stay. Aunty will go and bring her son from the school. We will play together."

I was trying hard to calm the child down when the doctor asked me, "What is he saying?"

I said, "No. Nothing. He just wants to go back home and play." Saying this, I quickly made for the gate when it did not escape my notice that she, my classmate, kept on standing there silently. She didn't open her mouth at all.

I felt so uneasy that I gave a faltering *namaskar* and left the place hurriedly.

The next morning the child was all right, and so I took him to the school. It was almost time. Others were returning leaving their children at the gate. My eyes rolled round looking for that lady, my classmate, and there she was coming back. She asked, "He is all right?" I smiled and nodded my head. I was just a few yards away from the gate. It might not have taken more than two to three minutes to leave the child at the gate, and the moment I turned back, I was surprised to see that she had gone far away by that time. What struck me was that she didn't smile while asking about the health of the child, and she was walking faster than the way she used to, as if she was trying to avoid me.

But why? Was it because that the mystery about the child had changed her impression of me?

Of course, it shouldn't matter anything to me now. What if she didn't smile? And also, what if she smiled? Why should she, after all?

I had no answer for such whys, but it made me sad. I felt extremely sad. I didn't feel like going home. It was not yet office time. I started wandering around.

When I came to my consciousness, I found myself in the midst of devastation. It was in fact a burning smell that brought me to consciousness. I saw myself there at the slum of my friend Santosh. Many of the materials of structures were lying scattered all over the ground: rough wooden poles, bamboos, torn tarpaulins, splintered tins, asbestos, corrugated sheets, and knotted jute-strings. Some burnt out, some half-burnt. Household things also like broken cots, earthen utensils, even tattered and burnt pieces of cloth, bed sheets, pillows, mosquito nets were laying higgledy-piggledy as one finds them on a cremation ground, smoke still coming out of smoldered wood and bamboos.

The whole scene had the look of a stretch of gloom. The smoke rising from the black ashes and smoldered bamboos, people passing by with a disdainful look and wry smile, children throwing stones and twigs into burnt out substances, and a strange sense of ruins and abandonment rendered the scene the look of a cremation ground. The pungently odd smell, as if of a burning dead body, moved me so deeply that I felt like crying out then and there. It was not so much the scene of ruins or demolition as the sense of a devastating abandonment, a harrowing feeling of an unfathomable emptiness, a dreadful shattering that started gnawing at my heart. I enquired about the old parents of my friend Santosh. Either I didn't get any response, or if there was a response, it was only a dumb expression and a sardonic smile.

Ultimately, defying the elders' warning, a boy told "They have left the place."

"Left? Where?"

"That we don't know," the boy said. Another boy, standing nearby said, "Must be from where they had come?"

When I came back home, it was not yet time to bring the child from the school. On my way home, I submitted in the office my application for leave.

In the loneliness of my room, I was sitting sadly holding the book I was writing. And, I discovered, it was there inside the manuscript the telegram that I had received long back. I felt the entire matter could be put like the way I had been putting other things in my book – the autobiography in the form of a fiction or the fiction in the form of an autobiography, whatever it may be, and so it goes:

The Death of My Mother

With the telegram in my hand, I was wondering, when there was a knock on the door. Keeping the telegram on the bed, carefully enough so that it didn't get lost anywhere, I opened the door, and the postman was there holding an envelop in his hand. I took it from him and shut the door and lying on the bed started reading the letter, a long one, from a relation of mine in the newly formed Bangladesh. It was a narrative kind of thing about the last days of my mother.

Your mother perhaps had gone insane. She didn't seem to be normal. Always pestering us to take her to her old house where she and your father used to stay and had to flee from in the darkness of a midnight on a fishing boat. And that was exactly what she used to recount over and again how you were born on a rutted wooden plank of that fishing boat flowing over the river Padma. She would go on recounting the same thing everyday, morning and evening, and would badger us for leading her to that old place for a visit, once, once only, at least to see how are those geese she had left behind at the backyard pond of their house, and because it was midnight and that in an unusually chaotic and violent situation she had to leave the place, and that, too, stealthily as if they were thieves or dacoits or criminals, so she even couldn't make out time to say goodbye to her fond geese, and that her geese might be wondering all these days where she (meaning your mother) had disappeared. One day it so happened that she went on fasting. Vowing that until she was helped to see her geese in the pond, she wasn't going to take food, and that compelled us one morning to lead her to her former place.

And there it happened, the tragedy, you may say. I don't know how exactly to express. In the early morning, we boarded a train, and it took a long time to locate the place finally around the late noon. Things have changed so vastly over these years that you cannot easily recognise the place you had seen twenty years or so back. The map of the place has changed, almost everywhere, roads, shops, market-areas, houses, structure of the houses, streets, connecting roads, paths, alleys, everything, even the residents, inhabitants. We reached the station, yes, there runs a train line there, and a small passenger halt has come up there just after the bridge constructed over the River Padma on whose flow you were born long back. We got down from the train, and it was really a scene to be seen that your mother created when we asked her to get down from the train there. She wouldn't. She would stay put to her seat in the compartment. Since the halting time was just two minutes, we tried to pull her out, but she went on resisting, denying that there was no railway halt in her place, and when all our attempts and coaxing failed, we had to physically lift her out. Coming out of the platform when again we forcibly made her sit on a rickshaw, rickshaw wasn't there…rickshaw wasn't there…you people are misleading me…misleading me…she kept on mumbling.

However, we reached the village, but then it was a hell of an affair to locate the exact house since the ownership of the house, as we were told, has changed from second to the third person, and that the main structure was completely a new one. First, your mother refused to accept it as her own former house, and then when she was convinced after lot of persuasion, she expressed happiness, and spreading a smile over her face, wanted to take a look at the backyard pond to which the wife of the present owner exclaimed, "Pond! No pond. It's filled up for this new structure."

At this, your mother was taken aback, literally. She was shocked to such an extent that you can't imagine. We simply noticed how shocked with wonder and fear full in her eyes she screamed, "And, where are my geese?"

"Geese?" The woman was surprised. "What geese?"

"Geese, my geese, I had left them in the pond."

The woman laughed. " Are you mad or what? When the pond is filled up how can there be geese there?"

And your mother kept on repeating, "But, what happened to my geese? I have to say them…" And, before she could complete, an old woman of around eighty or ninety with her back bending and resting her frail body on a stick came forward and said, " Hnaa, Hnaa! There were ducks and geese also… long back… long back… hnaa, I remember."

At this, your mother's face lit up, eyes sparkled, and in all excitement, she eagerly said, "Yes, yes, my geese, my geese, where are they?"

Raising her head a little, the old woman tried to look through her shrunken eyes at your mother and then smiled. "Arre! Pagli! Your geese were eaten up. There was a dawat that day. I remember. I remember, because it was me who cooked all the items. Lots of guests were there. I was then young, na. Not so old then as you see now. Back is bent. Hair gone white. So frail. Not like that. I cooked everything. Your geese I had cooked. Everybody appreciated, said very tasty, very tasty, all of them said."

By that time, your mother's eyes were closed. She was gradually fainting and slowly loosing her consciousness. Moments before she completely fell on the floor, she half opened her eyes trying to mumble, "Eaten up! Eaten…"

And, there she died. Anyway, at her own place.

I was sitting silently, feeling sad, looking blankly at my child intently playing with the building blocks, so peacefully, so happily, so securely with neither a bother nor a worry for what had happened or was happening to him. If parents are dead, so what? If not a single relation around, so what? No own house, no home – so what, kind of mind.

The child was totally engrossed in his game. It was then that there was a gentle knock on the door. I sat up and made for the door and on opening it thinking who it could be, I was surprised to see the lady, Neena as her doctor-husband told that day, my friend, standing at the door awkwardly. She smiled but looked very sad and as though eager to say something. Embarrassed, I, too, stood in silence for some time and then asked her to come in. Entering hesitantly, she raised her head and in a very unusually husky but soft tone said fumblingly, "I am sorry. No, no, please don't take it for a joke, I am really serious. Seriously speaking, I feel sorry. In fact, we didn't know. It was only today my relation, your psychiatrist-doctor, returned from Delhi, and from him, we came to know about you and your child. I am really sorry, and that's what I came for. Please, don't mind our behaviour that day. We were rude to you. I mean, we are very sorry."

I was so mystified by the whole situation that words failed me, and even I couldn't move either back or forward allowing her sufficient space to stand comfortably. As she was saying "sorry" her eyes looked tearful, her voice broke down, and she was so overwhelmed with emotion that before I could react, she suddenly held my hands tightly, passionately, and started crying loudly, shaking my hands violently and mumbling, "Sorry! I am sorry!"

An ecstatic thrill, an inexplicable sensation of a deep intimacy pulsating through my tissues ran over my whole body numbing my senses altogether.

I stood in dumb silence. Awestruck.

And then, all of a sudden, withdrawing her hands from my clasp with a heavy jerk, she went out of the room and almost ran away.

The Epilogue to My Book and the Prologue to My life

It was a Sunday morning, quite late of course, the winter, mid time between morning and the noon. The thick fog of the early morning was steadily clearing up for a hazy blue sky to be visible here and there in patches. The softness of a hesitant sunshine, a kind of cool in the air, and a leisurely ease in the Sunday atmosphere cast a spell of misty pleasantness all around.

My child was playing outside quite comfortably with other boys of the street. I was peeling potatoes to prepare a tasty *khichdi* for our midday meals when the child came running into the house.

"Auntie's coming! Auntie's coming! Doctor uncle's coming!" And following him, there they were, as if coming in a procession: the doctor uncle, Neena, my classmate friend, her doctor husband, all in smiles, looking cheerful and jolly.

I was surprised, couldn't decide what to do, where to make them sit. But, they didn't wait for my formal welcome. They straight away marched into my bedroom and made themselves extremely comfortable on my bed stretching their legs and reclining on my shabby pillows and folded quilt. My classmate friend Neena remained standing at the door. I pulled a stool from under the cot and gave it to her. She sat on it when her doctor husband said, "*Arre*! You sat down like a princess! As if attendants are there at your service!"

She looked at her husband, puzzled.

Her doctor-husband said, "Ah! You are really a stupid fellow." And then, waving his hand at us, he added in a tone of mock seriousness, "Now, you all be witness to my fate! How I have been managing my life with such a stupid fellow!"

It made all of us laugh heartily, including Neena, his wife, but still we were at a loss to get at the hint, the source of our laughter. He himself then made it clear, turning towards his wife. "My dear! Does it look nice to see that he makes tea for us?" And then he addressed me, "Well Mr! Go and show her the kitchen."

The child was playing outside, and we were all enjoying a cheerful late winter morning over hot tea and some *pakodas* that Neena, my classmate friend, prepared instantly and so deftly.

A relaxed, amiable, homely, fine cozy atmosphere. Hardly ever have I experienced all through my life. The sweet pleasantness of it started seeping through me.

Interrupting a joke that the psychiatrist was telling, Neena's doctor husband said to me, "Well! Well! Do you know the story of our marriage, Mr?"

"Story? What story?" I got curious.

But, she shut her husband's mouth up with her hand, pleading, "No, no, please, please don't."

At which her husband, still laughing, tried to remove her hand saying, "*Arre*! Let me tell your friend. What is there if told? It's not so ordinary a story after all?"

His wife resisted and then ultimately gave in, "All right, tell it, but no O Henry twist, mind it."

"All right; I will be absolutely faithful to events." With this reassurance her doctor husband started. "What happened you know? What happened *na* the very morning of our wedding-day we had the news that my so beloved would-be wife was missing!"

He paused and with a suppressed laughter glanced teasingly at his wife. But she, unembarrassed, waved her hand, nonchalant: "Carry on. Carry on. Don't stop in the middle."

"Yes, yes! Let's come back to our story." He resumed, "*Hnaa,* what was I telling? Missing. Yes, my would-be wife was missing, not found anywhere around, neither in her house nor in the town, and it was in the evening that one of her friends ... what was her name?" He asked his wife.

Unmoved, she said calmly, "Miss X."

"What?"

"Miss X," came the pat reply from her.

He picked up the thread of the story. "Yes, Miss X it was who rang up to inform that her friend, I mean, my beloved would-be wife had fled to the *ashram* of her Gurudev. What for? That, she didn't know. How could she come to know about it? No reply on the phone, silent. Now Mr! You can very well know that it was not necessarily for renunciation. No such stupidity after all."

Giving a mock slap on his back, she warned, "No comment permitted. Only the story as it is."

"Yes, madam! Yes, the narrator has no right to intrude into the events. Sorry for intrusion! Well! What happened then *na,* the whole platoon, platoon means our family members, their family members, our relations, their relations, our friends, their friends, even well-wishers, some known some unknown, the whole of the platoon reached the *ashram* the next day. Followed? And you see! It was like a grand procession of the wedding party. We reached the *ashram* and know what happened then?"

His wife raised her hand and asked him to stop. He stopped, wondering at his wife when she herself resumed, "That morning, I had the *darshan* of *Gurudev* alone. I touched his feet. *Gurudev* smiled and waved his hand to me to sit down. I was feeling nervous, tense. Once I sat down in front of him, a strange sensation ran through my whole body, and I started feeling relaxed, at home. I said, '*Gurudev*! I have fled from home.' He smiled, didn't say anything, but his bright eyes were fixed on me. I said, '*Gurudev*! I don't want to marry, and so I have fled from home.' This time also he just smiled, but his sparkling eyes were on me. I said, '*Gurudev*! I had a deep love for someone, but he couldn't even know it. What response to speak of!' I stopped abruptly and had no idea about what more to speak.

"*Gurudev* kept on smiling. Didn't say anything, but he was listening intently, each and every word. I said, '*Gurudev*! What should I do now?' Gurudev gave a smile and said softly, 'You see, the sun shines. If you keep your windows shut, you will be the unfortunate one not to get the light. Does it mean that the sun should stop giving light, because your windows are closed?' *Gurudev* paused for some moments, and then there was an expression, 'Umuuu?'

He made me contemplate what he said. And then, he resumed, 'It is in the nature of the sun to give light so that life will go on, and the moment the sun stops shining, it goes away from its nature, and it's no more the sun. It's something else but not the sun.' He again took a pause, and then, 'Umuu? Got it? Love is in our nature. To go away from love is to move away from our nature, and that is what is unnatural. It's then anything but not love. Give love like the sun giving light. Without sunlight, there cannot be life. Stop giving love, and you will no more be living. Umuuu?'

"I sat in silence for a long time, and then I bent forward to touch *Gurudev*'s feet. Gurudev placed his hand on my head and said, "Go, get married, be in love, and be in your nature. Let not life die.'"

She finished narrating her strange experience, raised her folded hands, and touched her forehead invoking her Gurudev.

There was complete silence in the room. The light, playful air of the beginning had given way to a serene atmosphere.

It was she, my classmate friend Neena, who broke the silence, looking at me. "Please, don't take it for a story."

***

No. I will not. I will not take your love for a story, my friend! I myself have been shuttling between the story and life, my novel and the reality. Even you were shuttling between the prologue of my book and my life, my dear friend! How can I deny it?

I have one essential thing to do now. I said to myself. It's the only thing I will go on doing till I make it happen. I decided.

Leaving my child in the school, I started walking straight to the police station. I will convince Santosh, my friend. Again and again. I will not let him wallow in the debris of history any more, to dream and die, like my mother. I will get him to come out to life, to be real and alive.

***

There is nothing called the logical conclusion. Man dies with his desires unfulfilled. Think of someone watching a TV series, and the series has just reached its climax, and the moment he is passionately waiting for what happens next, he dies of a sudden heart attack. What logic is there in such an end to his life?

If our real life fails to offer logic for its end, why should we then seek a logical end in our fiction? There is no end. Neither in life, nor in the book. It begins where it begins, and it ends where it ends.

Acknowledgements

i should like to thank Prof. Shiv K Kumar, the noted scholar writer, who first read a part of the manuscript and encouraged me to go ahead; Jake McPherson from New York, for editing the MS so diligently; Pravat Tripathy, a secluded poet in Hindi, for his insightful observations that had its way into the novel at different stages; Dr. Sudhansu S Mohanty, for his valuable suggestions on the initial draft.

i owe a lot to my student Mukteswar for his warmth and unwavering support at every stage of my writing.

i feel happy to remember the inspiration i used to get from Kalidash, Neelu babu and Nabaneeta.

i am indebted to my wife Susmita and my son Swagato, for the way they put up with my whims.

i am thankful to Sunil for taking up the publication of the novel.